Kim Wilson lives with her husband Wayne at the foothills of the beautiful Blue Mountains in New South Wales, Australia. She started writing quite late in life having started her career as an advertising copywriter and then continuing for the next twenty years as a fashion buyer! She married for the first time at the tender age of 57 so the last ten or so years have a complete turnaround for her. When she's not writing, she loves snow skiing, sailing, choral singing, her theatre group, reading (of course) and knitting! As well as copious amounts of tea wherever and whenever she can get it!

To Jean and Ron Welsh, my parents, who gave me a wonderful life and
always told me I could do anything I wanted to do.
Guess what? I did!
Thank you.

Kim Wilson

DANNY

AUSTIN MACAULEY PUBLISHERS™

LONDON * CAMBRIDGE * NEW YORK * SHARJAH

A CIP catalogue record for this title is available from the British Library.

ISBN 9781035812257 (Paperback)
ISBN 9781035813506 (ePub e-book)

www.austinmacauley.co.uk

First Published 2024
Austin Macauley Publishers Ltd®
1 Canada Square
Canary Wharf
London
E14 5AA

Once again, many thanks to my husband Wayne, to Maureen, to Dianee
and to Michael. You've all helped me enormously and given me
the courage to keep going!

Prologue

The rising sun casts a soft, apricot glow through the morning mist which is blanketing the fields and hedges of "Crofters Estate" in Much Hadham, Hertfordshire. The magic harmonies of early morning birdsong are only adding a final, welcoming touch to the day.

Summer has once again given way to autumn, so although this soft morning light presents a spectacular view, the pale yellow of the sun is a cruel mockery of its former golden self, radiating no warmth in its greeting, as numerous curling trails of smoke rising from the chimneys of the big house more than attest.

Owned by generations of the Fielding Family, the current owners, Philip and Priscilla Fielding, live mostly happy lives here with Philip working the land while Priscilla merely uses it as her "home base" between dashing to gala events in London, Los Angeles and Monte Carlo and fashion launches in Paris, Milan and Harrods, Knightsbridge.

Known by the nickname Priss, she is renowned in the county for her expansive hospitality and frequently has a houseful of friends for her famous weekend soirees, partying well into the night with Priss cementing her "hostess with the mostest" reputation, while Philip usually prefers to retire early and leave them to it.

He has never been the sociable type and really doesn't enjoy these frenetic parties, preferring a good book and a port in the nice quiet library any day but he doesn't mind Priss indulging, especially as he can see how happy it makes her.

The third member of their little family is their only child Daniel who is away at school all week at the prestigious Westminster School, only returning home every weekend to spend some well-earned time off with his beloved cows and farm animals.

But today he's indoors and standing wide-eyed as he shrinks back against the dining room door, trying with all his might to disappear. He's watching yet another loud, uncontrollable mob rampage through their beautiful home and can only think that this will be just another weekend down the drain.

His mother, he sees ruefully, is right in her element again. He's glad she's having fun, spending the weekend with her friends but she never has any time left for him! Doesn't he count for anything?

'Why on earth would Father let this continue?' he frowns up at Mrs Fisher, the housekeeper, 'I'll tell you why; because he's stuck in that damn library on his own all the time! He's got so many strangers taking over the rest of the house, he has no other option!'

'Watch your language, Master Daniel. Is that what they're teaching you at that posh school? And I think your father likes your mother to be happy, don't you?'

'Well yes, I do. Of course, I do but it can't go on like this forever! God, I wish you were my mother.' This is now such a familiar lament that Mrs Fisher has given up trying to tell him that it's not really the right thing to wish for.

'Daniel, language! Listen, why don't you go on up to your room for a while and have a look through your new history book? I'll bring you up some afternoon tea, a nice drink and a snack in about half an hour. What do you say to that?'

So, he once again heads desolately up the stairs and throws himself on his bed, as he grudgingly thanks his luck that at least he has his new book for company. He starts reading about the Boar War and decides that he'll sit with his father tonight and discuss it in depth.

His dad always has great insights into these things and can help him to understand what actually happened and the consequences better than any school teacher.

Before long, the weekend's gone and he's packed up and being whisked away back to school for another week. While he's always happy and eager to go back as he does miss his friends over the weekend, by the following Wednesday he is usually sitting in Latin class daydreaming about being back on the farm with his cows, chickens, a brood of snuffling hounds and his dad.

Some people would say he was torn between two worlds, always wanting the other but to his way of thinking, he has the best of both worlds and is the luckiest boy in the school.

He always has a ready answer to his teachers whenever they ask if he has a hobby and if so what is it? Easy, history! The farm is his way of life and will be *for the rest of his life but his one and only hobby is history. The other boys all snigger, of course.*

When asked, theirs are always the predictable sailing, skiing or pony riding. Normal, acceptable hobbies that they not only enjoy but allow them to be an integral part of their chosen group and birth given class. But they seem to miss the point.

History is his hobby but to him his first love and all he wants to do when he gets out of here next year, is work his father's farm. Full stop. He feels like that's why he was born and he also intends to keep the Fielding line well stocked with new little Fieldings before he is thirty.

His parents have already discussed Danny's future and have also come to the same conclusion. Prospective fifteen- to sixteen-year-old daughters from other well-to-do families are already being scouted and sorted into two distinct camps of possible and probable matches and a few are already firming up as front-runners.

Philip likes the Chisholm-Scotts' daughter as their land is adjacent to the Fielding Estate but of course, Priss prefers the Barbara and Ashley Hollingsworth heiress, as they are "frightfully rich", more so than the Chisholm-Scotts, and Babs is one of her closest friends and a fellow socialite about town.

The shrill ringing of the telephone in the hallway makes Priss physically jump in surprise as she happens to be standing right next to it, lost in deliberations about whether those windows need new drapes or not. Since there is no sign of Mrs Fisher or anybody else for that matter, she decides to answer it herself—something she would normally never do but she is expecting a call from Babs about the upcoming Charity Ball.

They are both on the committee and both feeling very grand, endlessly congratulating each other for their selfless but extremely tiring, charity work.

'Is that "The Darling of London Society"?' Babs teases with a twittering laugh.

'Oh, please, don't!' Priss answers in a tone that firmly implies—"Yes, definitely don't; don't stop, that is!" 'Can you believe that grubby little article? Whatever did I do to deserve their wrath like that?'

'Oh, no! I'd take it as a compliment—really, I would.'

Priss affects an embarrassed "if-you-say-so" air and they start to discuss the ball. To Priss' delight, Babs tells her that the Robertsons will be over from

Australia and just in time for the festivities. She invited them on the spot, of course, and told Janet to make sure she packs her favourite ball gown!

But if she can't fit it in, the three of them could always have a girls' shopping day while her Daryl goes off to talk about his dreary sheep with the other men. Priss secretly hopes she doesn't bring a gown—there's nothing she likes better than a day's shopping and lunching with the girls.

'Anyway, I thought maybe we could dress the tables with Australian Wattle and those little leaves the Koalas eat. What are they called? Oh, it doesn't matter. I have a fabulous florist who can manage all that and he'll know, no trouble!' Babs enthuses.

'What a lovely idea! A colonial theme! Oh and make sure you put us on the same table, please. I know Philip really enjoys a good, long chat with Ashley and Daryl of course when he's over.'

With that organised, the girls move on to the more salacious gossip of the day.

*

The night of the ball finally arrives and Priss comes down the staircase looking like a Parisian model in a beautiful yellow gown of crystal and gold, a sprig of wattle accentuating her tiny waist. She's definitely not going to be upstaged by any amount of bloody wattle on a dining table!

But she didn't want to clash either. And she's right, she's outshining the rich, Australian, golden wildflowers by a mile! Next to her, the extravagant, sparkling table centres and floral displays fade into the background and take on the appearance of mere weeds. "The darling of London's society" is in full swing tonight.

'A touch of our darling Queen's Australian portrait? Very cheeky!' says Babs when she sets her eyes on her. Trying to sound enthusiastic, she only comes across as jealous and just a touch petty. She looks down at her classic black number and cringes. Maybe "classic" just isn't her style!

'I don't know what you mean!' Priss demurs.

'Yellow gown? Wattle at the waist?'

'Well, darling, your man has done such a fabulous job with the tables, I didn't want to clash with them; rather pay an homage to the wonderful artistry!'

With Babs mollified, the two women sit at the table and comfortably proceed to rip shreds off all the other women in the room.

Once the formality of dinner is finished, Philip and Daryl sit back and enjoy some port and cigars while their wives hop from table to table, accepting the multitudinous congratulations with blatantly false modesty. Presently, the subject of their sons comes up.

The boys are the same age, sharing the same ambition to take on the family farms when they leave school and both are looking at courses that will help them with all the modern techniques and may even provide some hands-on experience at the same time.

'Hands-on is definitely the thing; don't you think, Daryl?'

'Absolutely. You can only learn so much about farming from a book. You have to get your hands dirty, live through the droughts, fires and floods and come out the other side ready to do it all again. And you need to do that to really understand what it's all about, don't you think?'

Philip frowns, deep in thought as he empties his glass and signals to a waiter for a refill. 'Daniel will never get that kind of experience here, we just don't have those natural disasters at the rate you do! But I suppose we do have other challenges to keep us busy.'

Daryl turns to Philip, thanking the waiter as he does, 'Paul has lived through so many in his short lifetime that he just thinks of them as the norm.' He pauses and takes a sip. 'Tell you what. What would you think about swapping the boys for a year? A student exchange if you like? I think learning all the different methods for the different conditions would be invaluable to both of them and being away from us at this point of their lives will give them a certain sense of independence as well. What do you say?'

Philip draws on his cigar and offers his hand to seal the deal.

*

And so, six weeks later, Daniel finds himself walking out of the airport in Dubbo, New South Wales into the brightest, clearest sunshine he's ever seen. It's still only spring but to him, the heat is stifling and he feels rather overdressed in his tweed suit and knitted vest. He stands, looking around in bewilderment.

What is he supposed to do now? He has the address of the farm so decides to take the initiative and get a cab that will show them that he can think for himself and doesn't need to be shepherded along every step of the way. The cabbie jumps obligingly out of the driver's door and pops the boot to stash Daniel's luggage and with an almighty heave, he is just lifting his heavy bag off the ground when he hears his name being called.

He swings around to find a beautiful, smiling young girl looking happily at him, with two young, identical boys jumping up and down by her side. She laughs and asks what on earth he thinks he's doing.

'I'm just taking a cab to the Robertson's place,' he says, dropping the bag back down on the footpath in embarrassment.

'Well, I'm Cheryl Robertson and you're not doing anything of the sort. We've just driven all this way to get you and that's exactly what I'm going to do.' She laughs again and apologises to the confused taxi driver while scooping Danny's heaviest bag up as if it's no heavier than a bag of groceries.

'Twins!' Daniel laughs, looking down on their blonde heads.

'Yes, double the trouble! Don't let their angelic faces fool you though; beneath that unruly mop of blonde hair, they're a couple of little monsters!' The boys make loud, scary monster noises at him and he pretends to jump back terrified but he can't help laughing out loud.

'How old are they?'

'Three and a half! They start school next year and I for one can't wait!'

'Hello, boys. What's your names?'

'I'm Ian and he's Alan. What's your name?' They both snigger.

'I'm sure you know it already; my name is Daniel but all the kids at my school used to call me Danny, so I think that one would be better, don't you?' They both nod their heads silently.

'Come on, let's get over to the car. And you two mind your manners.' Cheryl shakes her head as if she's just about given up. 'How was your trip, anyway? Bloody long way!'

Quietly taken aback by her casual swearing, he tells them all about his flight as they walk over to a dusty but relatively new Jeep and they all climb in, boys in the back and Danny in the passenger seat. Cheryl insists on driving as she "knows the road" and the boys cackle with laughter. 'Nobody's allowed to drive her precious car!' Ian teases to Alan's great amusement.

'Shut up, Ian! And you too, Alan!'

'No, you shut up!'

'Enough!' Danny says in a commanding voice looking with raised eyebrows at Cheryl. She would later tell him that it was this moment and that look that won her heart.

But right now, they all settle down ready for the long drive out to "Whitegum Station" where Danny will be spending the next year.

He's heard the scenery is beautiful out there but stealing another sideways glance at Cheryl, he thinks it will have to go a long way to beat the scenery in here!

Chapter One
Jake-2011

Laughter, shouting and what sounds like the chattering of monkeys, echoes all around the playground as seven-year-old Jacob McMullen sits on his favourite bench eating his cheese and tomato sandwich and trying to juggle both his lunchbox and drink bottle on his lap at the same time.

He looks up, through the branches and shivering leaves of the towering gum tree above him to a beautiful, sun kissed clear blue sky; he loves this view and he revels in it until his gaze is drawn back down to the playground around him.

At the moment, it's full of rampaging children and he watches them quietly, his eyes skipping from group to group noticing that they're either sitting in their groups eating, running around aimlessly or playing handball with their mates and then he looks sorrowfully at the empty space next to him on the bench.

This spot had until recently been occupied by his best friend, Simon Easterbrook but his family had moved away to some faraway place that Jacob had never even heard of. Why they had to do that, he would never understand.

So, here he is on his own and he supposes he'd better just get used to it. He and Simon were always known as "The Geeks" and they'd been more than happy with that, sticking together and seeming to exist in their own little world. But now he was just "The Geek" and that was a lonely place to be.

'Hey! Baby Jake ate a snake and it gave him a stomach-ache! Poor little Baby Jake,' comes the now familiar, taunting chant. Robbie Smythe had thought that little gem up all by himself and since then the other boys have always joined in cheerfully whenever the opportunity presented itself.

'What's the matter, *Baby Jake*? Got no little friend to keep you comp'ny anymore? Boo-hoo!'

He's about to tell Robbie and his mates to get lost but then hears his mother's voice clearly in his ear. 'Ignore them, darling. They're just jealous. Honestly, they're not worth your time and effort.' So, he tries his best to do just that but there's no use pretending.

Their incessant chanting does hurt and upset him, especially when there are a group of *them* and only one of *him*. He feels his eyes tearing up and is mortified by the thought that if they see that, it will only give them yet another thing to pick on.

'Give it a break! Leave him alone!' comes an unfamiliar voice, cutting through the taunts and insults. 'Go on, rack off, all of you!'

Jake looks up in surprise and sees a strange boy standing in front of him. He's never seen this boy before so why is he helping him? He's wearing a different uniform to the rest of them and as he stands feet apart and hands on his hips, he directs an angry, menacing growl towards Robbie and his cohorts.

'Kenneth Walker.' He holds his hand out like a grown man for Jacob to shake. 'But you can call me Kenny.' Jacob looks up to the boy feeling ridiculously grateful.

'Thank you, my name is Jacob McMullen but everyone just calls me Jake.' And that's the start of a roller coaster lifelong friendship.

He sits next to Jake and starts exploring the contents of his own lunchbox. Why did he even bother to look? His mother has given him the same lunch every day of his school life and he's good and tired of it. Does she eat the same thing for lunch every day herself? No way!

'Aww, not curried egg again! Every day, I'm sick to death of it.'

Jake smiles, he has the same problem. He wishes he'd never told his mother how much he loved the cheese and tomato, extra salt and pepper, sandwich she gave him on his first day at big school.

He sympathises with Kenny and after a mutual complaint session about their boring mothers, they decide to try swapping every second day until they get sick of that. At least it's easier than trying to talk to their mothers about it.

'Not that I'm scared of my Mum, of course,' Kenny blurts out defensively.

'Of course.' Jake smiles at his new lunch buddy and heads down, they both proceed to empty their crammed lunchboxes into their empty, growling stomachs. With that task accomplished, Kenny turns to Jake and looking at him thoughtfully, wants to know what those guys were doing when he came up just then.

Shrugging his shoulders, Jake tells him that they've always been like that but it's got a lot worse since his best friend Simon left and *he* was left sitting on his own.

'Don't worry about that anymore, mate. I'm here now and I can take care of any of those lily-livered cowards single-handed, if they're game to have a go!'

*

At first, they just spend their time getting to know each other. But as their friendship grows, they start going to each other's homes for a meal or a sleepover. Jake's Mum, Diana seems uncharacteristically wary of Kenny though; she's noticed his wandering eyes taking in all their prized possessions, not appreciating the beauty or age of the antiques but almost as if he's appraising each item for its value and saleability.

'You have some beautiful things, Mrs McMullen,' Kenny would say, sidling up to her in an effort to curry her favour and Jake would beam at his mother. How can she not like his new best friend when he is always complimenting the things she loves most? 'You have exquisite taste!'

Exquisite? Diana thinks, what little boy his age uses such language and how on earth would he know the difference anyway? She decides to ask around the other school mothers to see what she can learn about this new family. She wants to know their background and what brought them here in the first place. After all, Jacob could end up spending some serious time with them.

'I'm not totally sure about this new friend of Jacob's,' she says to her husband Geoffrey one night after he's driven Kenny home.

'Is that why I'm relegated to drive him home every time he comes for dinner now instead of them having a sleepover?'

Something in the tone of her husband's voice tells her that he doesn't feel the same way. 'Well, yes. I know it sounds silly and I've really nothing to go on except a couple of stray comments he's made but I just don't feel comfortable with him and don't want him under our roof overnight. Call it women's intuition.'

'Diana, he's only seven years old. Get a grip on yourself, woman.'

She's taken aback at the tone of his voice, sometimes he's so patronising but maybe he's right, maybe I'm just an overprotective mother hen but I really wish Simon was still around. There was never any trouble then. She knows that Jacob misses his friend enormously too but she's learned not to mention anything about it to either Jacob or his father as Jacob only gets upset and Geoffrey snaps her head off.

'And before you say it, don't bring Simon into it again.' Looks like he'll snap her head off anyway, even when she doesn't mention him. Will he ever be able to speak civilly to her again? 'Now for God's sake, stop worrying and go to sleep!' And there's the answer to that question.

He rolls over in a huff, turns out his bed lamp and is snoring contentedly within a few minutes, leaving Diana to stare at the dark ceiling and fret.

*

Diana's constant worrying soon proves to be warranted though, when one sunny afternoon not long before her son's eighth birthday, she takes a call from the principal of Jacob's school.

'Mrs McMullen. Sorry to disturb you but this is John Sanderson, Principal of Lakeside Primary. We've had a bit of a problem with young Jacob today and I was wondering if you're able to come down and collect him this afternoon so we can have a little chat about what's happened?'

'A problem? Is Jacob alright?'

'Yes, yes, he's fine; nothing to worry about there. I'd just like to have a word with you. How does 2:30 sound?'

'Oh, of course, that's fine. I'll be there and thank you, Mr Sanderson.'

2:30 can't come quickly enough for Diana as numerous scenarios run amok through her fertile imagination. What on earth could have happened? Jacob's a good boy, surely there's been a mistake. Has he accidentally damaged something? If he did, they'd pay to have it fixed, of course. Her mind jumps to the "obvious" conclusion; he's going to be suspended or even worse, expelled!

All the way to the school she worries that she should have called Geoffrey to meet her there and deal with it but she really couldn't stand the scene he would cause. She determines to take control of this one herself and hopefully, present Geoffrey with not only the problem but also the solution at the same time! She'll show him she's not as useless as he always seems to believe.

Arriving at the principal's office just as 2:30 ticks over on the large school clock, she mentally crosses off the first item on her To Do list; to be punctual and not keeping the headmaster waiting. Expecting a secretary or something, she's a bit non-plussed to find that there's nobody around to help her, so she knocks nervously on the door which swings open almost instantly giving her a bit of a shock. Has he been standing there waiting for her? She looks up at the rather tall and imposing gentleman looming over her.

'Mrs McMullen, thanks for coming.' He ushers her inside and motions to the front of his desk for her to take a seat. He's never had to have this sort of conversation with the McMullens and as he takes his own seat behind the old glass top mahogany desk, he casts an eye over the impeccably groomed and poised woman sitting opposite him.

The only thing that gives away how she is feeling is a nervous crease between her brows and her hands clasped so tightly in her lap that her knuckles have turned white.

'My pleas—oh, I was going to say my pleasure but obviously it's not that at all, is it?' Diana answers confused and just wanting to get it all over with.

'No, unfortunately, it's not!'

'What is it? What's happened?'

'Look, I'll get straight to the point. I'm afraid young Jacob was caught stealing from the school canteen at lunchtime today. It seems he'd thrown his own lunch in the bin when he decided that the canteen food looked much more appetising.'

Diana gasps, feeling inadequate and absurdly guilty as if she's sure he'll think she doesn't feed her son properly and she looks just as guilty as she feels. She needs to take control of herself. Never! Never in her life has she been confronted with something like this. She feels so ashamed that her son was actually stealing food!

She needs to refocus and get a bit more clarity. But why would he do that? She opens her mouth and is about to ask him another question when they both look up simultaneously as a tentative knocking at the principal's door interrupts the flow of their conversation.

'Enter,' he calls in a louder, more authoritative tone than he'd hitherto been using.

The door opens slowly and there, shaking in the doorway is Jake. He knows he's in for it now; he just doesn't know what "it" will be! This is the first time he's been in trouble and so far, he's not liking it at all. He wishes he'd just eaten his stupid sandwich and not listened when Kenny told him they shouldn't have to eat those dull old things again when there's a tuckshop full of yummy stuff for them to feast on.

He'd made it sound so exciting and empowering as he'd planned how they were going to get their hands on the said feast and so full of common sense that in the end, it didn't even feel like stealing! After all, Kenny had reassured him, they just throw all the leftover food in the bin at the end of lunchtime anyway and you can't steal from the garbage, can you? It's just there to be taken! All they're doing is taking it before it gets germs all over it from being in the grotty old bin!

Jake surveys the scene and feels his stomach tighten when he sees his own mother sitting there. Mr Sanderson beckons for him to come in and take the seat next to his mother.

He sits down carefully, balancing on the edge almost as if he needs to be ready to run and looks hard at his mother's face to see if he can find any clue from her as to what he can expect. But all he sees is disappointment and that's the hardest thing of all to accept.

'Well, what have you got to say for yourself?'

'I'm sorry,' he mumbles into his chest.

'I'm sorry *what*?'

'I'm sorry, *sir*?' Jake hates it when he has to play this guessing game with adults. Why do they always do that? At least the answer with his mother is always 'please'! But that doesn't seem to be the best thing to say right here and now.

Mr Sanderson shakes his head and tries a different tack.

'What are you sorry *for*, Jacob?'

'For stealing food from the tuck shop, sir and I'm sorry Mum, for throwing my lunch in the garbage bin.'

'That's alright, darling. But I don't know how alright it's going to be with your father when he gets home.' Jake's face blanches and his stomach does somersaults; for a moment, he'd totally forgotten about his dad and his vile temper!

Mr Sanderson clears his throat. He delivers a pointed and very clear message to "young Jacob". He turns to him, frowning, 'You've always been a top pupil, Jacob. I just can't understand why you would ever do something like this. I'm *very* disappointed in you and I sincerely hope this incident is a one off.'

Jake's head drops like a naughty puppy being scolded.

The principal continues, 'But I think this time and only this time, we can leave this whole sorry episode there. Instead, I'll let your parents decide what the appropriate punishment should be, except,' and he looks over his glasses to make his point understood, 'that you are banned from going anywhere near the tuckshop for one whole week. Do you understand? And if you don't want to be in any bigger trouble than you already are, you'll do well to remember it. No tuckshop for the next week.'

'Yes, sir. Thank you, sir.' Even to his own ears, he sounds grovelling but he can't trust himself to say another word, not the way he is feeling at the moment. He is told to wait in the corridor while his mother and Mr Sanderson finish up their conversation and he immediately jumps up, standing straight and tall, hoping that he's giving the impression that he is willing to bend over backwards to do as he is asked before he shoots out of the room like a bullet from a gun, not needing to be asked twice.

Diana looks distraught, 'I'm so sorry for this, Mr Sanderson. I don't know what's got into him. We don't starve him, you know, he eats like a horse at home. But I'll definitely get to the bottom of this and I'll make sure it doesn't happen again!'

'Don't be too hard on yourself or him, Mrs McMullen. All kids will try to push their luck from time to time. Jacob's always been a model student and I know he's been floundering a bit since the Easterbrooks left. He really misses Simon and that can only be mended with time. If anything further happens, we'll be in touch.'

He stands and buttons up his jacket as he walks around the desk to escort her out, making Diana feel like she'd just been to the doctors and he was ready for his next patient.

'Thank you again for coming in.'

As she walks out to Jacob, she sees another world-weary mother sitting on the bench next to him. Mr Sanderson greets her. 'Mrs Walker.'

Mrs Walker stands up sluggishly and turns to Jake. 'See ya, Jake.'

'See ya, Mrs Walker.'

'I told ya, call me Fay.' She walks into the office and the door closes firmly behind her.

'You'll do no such thing! You do *not* call an adult by their Christian name, show some respect!' Diana takes Jake's bag from him wondering how he ever carries this thing, it's so heavy.

She knows it's time for a serious chat. So, she takes the opportunity of being alone with him in the car to talk to him about what happened today and why. He tells her it only happened because he doesn't like the same sandwiches every day. But he looks so apologetic while he's finally telling her, that she feels terrible he didn't feel he could come to her about it before!

They're only sandwiches! And he adds, sometimes he doesn't eat anything at all rather than even try to eat them again! Diana feels awful hearing this, she'd always thought they were his favourites, so on the way home they stop at the shops to stock up on sandwich fillings to tide him over until her next big shop.

As anticipated, Geoffrey hits the roof and Jake is hit with a torrent of abuse and accusations until Diana steps in and points out to her raving husband that it's all been said before and together, she and Jacob have found a solution to the problem, so as far as she's concerned it's now "case closed".

*

Things roll along very quietly after this with Kenny being banned from their home for the same week as the tuckshop ban and after the next few months have passed, the incident is all but forgotten. Until—

The following year, Diana is called back into the principal's office.

Jake and Kenny had started a class riot with all the children stomping their feet and chanting, 'We won't do it, we don't have to!' when they'd been asked to help tidy the classroom. They all went totally crazy, kicking over any furniture they were not already jumping on and running around the normally peaceful classroom, screaming and shouting uncontrollably.

This time Mr Sanderson was not so forgiving and Jake suspected, neither would his father be. They both earned another week's suspension but this time, it was a total suspension from the school itself, not just the tuckshop. Back at home, Geoffrey rages, Diana pleads to know why and Chelsea stays in her room.

Jake takes it all quietly and retreating to his own room, he silently congratulates himself on his week off. He's convinced a break from that place is just what he needs.

Coming out to breakfast the next morning, Diana is surprised to see a huge smile on his face. Gone is the remorseful, penitent little boy from last night and she can only attribute this to the resilience of youth. He informs her that he has grand plans for this week now that he is free of having to go to that crummy school every day and excitedly starts outlining them all to his mother. But he's surprised and very quickly disappointed at her reaction.

'Oh no, you're not! You're *banned* from *going* to school as a punishment, you're *not* on holiday. You'll be in third class soon and you still have your yearly tests coming up. So just settle down and get stuck in, Jacob. I've set up your books for you on your desk in the family room, there's good light in there so you should be right. And I expect you to double down in light of why you're in there. I won't stand for any more of this carry on!'

*

The next two to three years limp along peppered with various incidents which the school and the family have to deal with but with growing impatience and anger. Each time, the punishment becomes harsher and the boys grow more and more rebellious.

When it finally comes time for Jake to start high school, he is taken by surprise when Geoffrey sits him down one night and tells him that he won't be going to the local high school with all the other boys next year. He can't have this rambunctious behaviour continuing through the next six years of his schooling.

'Your mother and I have discussed it and we think you need to go somewhere with a strict hand as well as top educational qualifications. So, you'll be going to St Patrick's Lakeside. There is no room for argument, you're already enrolled and that's the end of the discussion.'

Jake races up the stairs, tears streaming down his face and throws himself onto his bed, cursing, swearing and fist-pumping his pillow.

*

His first day in his new school proves to be confusing and unsettling. He's suddenly gone from being the big boy in the school to being very, very small fry here. The only thing that makes him happy but his parents decidedly unhappy, is the familiar cocky, smiling face staring back at him from across the room in their welcome assembly.

Kenny! Jake pushes his way through the other boys to him and stands by his side. And on that day, to Jake at least, all seems right with the world.

It doesn't take them long to fall back into their old routine and their troublemaking continues through the years there, with two notable incidents even leading to the police being called which saw the two of them end up in front of the Juvenile Court.

The first, when they were both fourteen, was downright dangerous. They set fire to some papers in a garbage bin resulting in them being charged with wilfully damaging property and putting lives at risk. Jake stands in the court before the magistrate, who looks more like a caring grandmother than a strict judicial officer and looks over to his parents; his expression telling them just how scared and very sorry he is.

The magistrate asks if he has anything he would like to say for himself and he immediately puts on his best "sorry puppy" face and tells her that they didn't think through the consequences of their actions. They just wanted to see if they could set off the smoke alarms because another boy had told them that none of the school's smoke alarms really worked.

As this was his first time before the court, he was given a stern warning and sent home with his parents, where he was obviously yelled at and grounded for a month except to go to school. Both boys were on their first warning with the school as well, so they laid low for a long while after that.

But one day, not long after Jake's fifteenth birthday, the two boys decide that they're never going to need science when they leave school so, during their interminable double science lesson, they agree to "borrow" the gardener's four-wheel trolley cart and try their luck at Trolley Luge down the steep driveway of the teachers' carpark.

They soon reach dizzying speeds but with no way to steer the "stupid thing" or stop it for that matter, they soon come undone crashing into Mr Johnston's comfy old Mazda 3, caving the door in and scraping the paint right back to the metal.

'Kenny, look what you've done!' Jake screams loud enough for the whole school to hear. Kenny stands up, dusting his pants off and together they do the only thing they can think of and hightail it out of there before the damage to the car is discovered. But to their horror, Mr Johnston is just walking up the driveway to get his jacket from his car and meets them head on.

This time the school is not kidding around with their punishment and their parents are told that this might not be the best school for the boys after all; could they please find somewhere else for them to go?

Back in the Juvenile Court again, Jake is standing trying to sum up the new magistrate before him. Gone is the kindly grandmother figure and in her stead is a grim, frowning and stern-faced "old geezer" who looks like he won't stand for any silly business at all.

At the end of the day, with Jake nervously grovelling his way through his testimony, he is given a suspended sentence of three months and his second warning. He is also ordered to pay for the damages to Mr Johnston's car and is sent home, his tail between his legs with the words of the magistrate still ringing in his ears.

'If you break the terms of this suspension, you will be straight back here. Do you understand?' Jake understands only too well and decides to take what was given and keep his mouth shut, no matter what.

He travels home with his parents that day in an awkward silence and endures another lecture from his father, his mother seeming to have given up after last year's fiasco.

*

The McMullens meet with Mr and Mrs Walker and decide the best thing for both boys will be to separate them for the remainder of their schooling. Jake heads off to a new private school, thanks to the strings his father can pull and Kenny is sent to the local high school, his parent's deciding that his interest in learning doesn't warrant the money they would have to pay out on further private education.

Jake settles into this new school remarkably well and is taking a lot from his new and uninterrupted flow of learning. Periodically, Diana would see Mrs Walker at the local shopping centre and from what she says, Kenny has been reacting just as positively to his new environment as Jake has to his.

The boys stay in touch with phone calls and the "new-fangled" social media sites as Diana refers to them, even though they've been around for aeons. She's in the lounge one afternoon watching a re-run of her favourite cooking show when Jake walks nervously in.

'Mum, it's Mrs Walker's birthday tomorrow and she's having a bit of a party tomorrow night. Do you think Dad would let me go? She wants me to stay the night because Mr Walker will be drinking and won't drive after he's had a couple.'

Diana knows they've both been behaving and their grades have been improving as well. What harm could one night over at Kenny's do? So, she agrees and talks Geoffrey around after dinner that night. The next day is Saturday, so while Jake excitedly packs a bag, she goes down to the shops and buys Mrs Walker a bunch of flowers for Jake to give her, along with a card.

Geoffrey isn't thrilled that she'd all but agreed to Jake going before talking to him about it but she argues, you can't lock him up forever and he hopes Jake just might have second thoughts about renewing the friendship when he actually sees Kenny again. Things do change and so far, this change has definitely been for the better, with Kenny nowhere in sight.

They're settled comfortably that night, sitting with their mugs of hot chocolate and watching their favourite weekly cops and robbers show on the television when the phone rings.

'Oh, Mrs McMullen? It's Fay Walker here. I was just wondering if I could talk to Kenny for a minute, please.'

Diana's confused. 'Kenny? But isn't he there? Jacob's staying over there tonight for your birthday!'

Now it's Fay Walker's turn to be confused. 'My birthday's in April! Kenny told me he was staying at Jake's. That you had invited him over for a roast dinner and as Mr McMullen doesn't like to drive after he's had a couple of drinks, he would stay the night.'

The two mothers spend the rest of the night lying awake and worrying about their sons while their husbands fume and plot their punishments, each allowing a tiny bit of worry to creep in, almost unacknowledged through the clouds of their angry disappointment.

'I love thish kinda,' he wiggles his finger up at the sky trying to remember the word. 'Shky! Shame to go inshide.' And it is, the dawn is breaking and the sky is absolutely spectacular. As he opens the door, it lets out a loud "creak!" which echoes through the sleeping home and he turns to it frowning, fingers to his lips.

'Shoosh!' comes the drunken instruction but the door remains stubbornly squeaky on its hinges. He stops and thinks hard trying to remember the story he and Kenny had cooked up about why he's home so early and giving up on that, he opens the refrigerator door. The overhead light snaps on, flooding the kitchen in bright white light and he jumps a mile, yelling 'hey!' before spinning around in confusion only to be confronted by the angry faces of both his mother and Father.

No allies here today then. His mother bursts into tears of relief that he's home safe, her anger immediately forgotten but his father's anger quickly escalates until it develops into a stone-cold rage, the kind he can't be talked down from.

He knows that this time he's gone too far. He's slapped with a ten o'clock curfew for the rest of his school years; his father wishes it could be for the rest of his life and if he's not home before the clock in the hall strikes ten, they will immediately ring the police to report it. Then he can see for himself how that sits with his illustrious record!

To Jake, this is the living end. From that moment on, all communication between him and his parents breaks down and if he's spoken to directly, he does answer but only with a grunt before disappearing upstairs and into his room, music blaring.

Life in their household becomes increasingly difficult, the atmosphere charged with electric tension and stress ready to discharge at a moment's notice with the merest word or sideways glance. With Jake having to account for every move he makes, he feels humiliated and belittled and the worst thing is, he knows he only has himself to blame!

Chapter Two
Monday-St Ives, Sydney

'Where do you think you're going?' Geoffrey McMullen barks at his 18-year-old son Jacob, glaring over the rim of his reading glasses at the retreating back of his son.

'*Out*! Not that it's any of *your* business,' he adds under his breath.

'Have you been drinking *again*? It'd better not be my good whisky, the way you swill it down, it's a damn waste of a bloody good drop.' Too many times lately, Geoffrey's picked up the bottle to find it half empty *again*. He sits fuming at Jacob's impertinence and thinks that he still can't come to grips with the change in him over the last few years.

He was always such a happy-go-lucky and even-tempered kid but since all the troubles at school, he's totally transformed into a defiant and angry teenager; forever bickering and fighting with both him and his mother, drinking and taking God knows what else behind the barricaded door of his bedroom or out every night with his "mates".

But when he started staying out late every other night, even on one noteworthy occasion not coming home at all, action was needed. He thought he'd put a stop to that quick-smart by giving him a curfew but he's still having trouble curbing Jacob's surly, rebellious attitude and Jacob takes no heed of the curfew at all. He's sure it all started with Simon leaving in primary school and Jacob picking up with that Kenneth Walker!

Jake, he's now come to hate the name 'Jacob', turns to his father, incandescent with rage. '*Will. You. Please. Stop. Treating. Me. Like. A. Child*? There, can I be any *clearer* for you? I'm *18* years old now and I can drink whatever I like, with or without your permission.'

'*NOT MY WHISKY, YOU CAN'T!*' his father bellows back at him, on the verge of losing all control over his own ever-ready temper. Maybe the son is more like the father than the father would like to believe!

'Well, can I drink your *milk* then? Or do I need permission for that too?'

Geoffrey advances on Jacob, fists clenched and eyes bulging. 'Smart Ar—'

'Yeah, come on, old man. Think you can take me on. Do ya?'

'*STOP IT! STOP IT, PLEASE!*' Diana cries out in anguish. Stepping in between them, she has her hands over her ears and tears streaming down her face. 'I can't *stand* this anymore. For God's sake, JUST STOP IT!'

They both freeze in their tracks and Jake looks at his mother in surprise. She's been turning her back on these scenes for a long time now, usually leaving them to sort it out between themselves and this turn of events today is both emotional and very worrying for both of them.

Geoffrey turns on his heel and storms out of the room saying he's going to check on Chelsea. Jake's younger sister had fled the room as the fight was brewing and is now sheltering in her bedroom with her indecipherable music blaring full blast to blot out the terrifying sounds; a trick she'd learned from her big brother, leaving Diana and Jake staring at each other in shocked silence.

'Why do you have to do that, Jacob? I know you're a good boy deep down but I can't understand why you feel you need to behave like that all the time. Haven't we given you everything you've ever needed?'

It seems that last question is enough to spark Jake's settling anger right back up again. '*Yes, Mum!* You've *given* me every *material* thing I've *ever* needed.' But what he doesn't say is that all he ever really wanted as he grew was their support, something he'd always felt was badly lacking.

'I'm my own person you know and right now all I actually need is to get out of this bloody hell hole before I go mad.' And with that, he storms out of the house, leaving his mother upset and totally confused. What did she say now?

*

Diana and Geoffrey

1996

It hadn't always been like this. When Geoffrey McMullen met Diana Volkert in 1996 at a friend's wedding, he was instantly smitten. She was the most beautiful girl he'd ever seen and her friend Sally, who'd married his best friend Rob couldn't be happier, she'd known from the first time she'd met Geoffrey that these two would hit it off and she was right!

Their friendship blossomed right from the start and soon they were dating steadily, either double dating with Sally and Rob or spending time alone together with romantic nights involving just the two of them, a bottle of champagne and the twinkling stars above.

'When are we going to meet this young fellow of yours?' Diana's mother constantly asked. Actually, she was getting so tired of asking, that she even hated hearing herself utter the words!

'Well, I was thinking of inviting him over for lunch on Sunday, if that's alright? We are having a roast, aren't we? I'd love him to taste your roast lamb! We'd both rather have good old-fashioned plain food than all the new beans and sprouts stuff they serve up these days!'

Marion Volkert raises her eyebrows at these last affectations! We both? When did they become a 'we' and when did Diana start speaking like that? And talk about a backhanded compliment! "Good old-fashioned plain food"? For heaven's sake, Diana's always loved her Sunday Roast; lamb, chicken or pork!

'Well, I'm glad you both love good old-fashioned plain food because that's all you're ever going to get here!'

'Mum, I didn't mean it like that!' Major eye roll for effect, 'you know what I mean, stop being so precious!'

'I will as soon as you pull your horns in and drop all the airs and graces! And yes, of course it's alright to ask him over! You know your friends are always welcome here! What's his name anyway?'

'It's Geoffrey, Geoffrey McMullen and he's nearly finished his Medical Degree but he still can't decide what to specialise in. He's tossing up between Obstetrics and Gynaecology. He's extremely clever!' Her mother shakes her head and walks out of the room hoping that he's not as stuck up as her daughter's becoming, apparently thanks to his influence.

The next Sunday morning is a flourish of activity in the Volkert household. Diana is absolutely determined to impress Geoffrey with a full table service of fine china, bone handled cutlery which is only brought out once or twice a year for special occasions; actually Christmas has been the only occasion for the last few years and crystal glassware on which she's already spent a full hour rubbing and polishing until it's throwing out dazzling lights all the colours of the rainbow.

Even the white damask tablecloth is getting an airing and Diana's father William laughs at the sight of the sparkling but weighed down table in their modest, comfortable home. 'Who's coming to lunch? The Queen?'

Marion shakes her head in the kitchen, 'No luv, it's just the new boyfriend!'

'Mother! Don't say it like that! You make it sound like there's a new one every week! And besides, Geoffrey's special. You'll like him. I know you will. Both of you!'

Her father salutes her thinking, 'Yes Sir, Sergeant Major!' just as the doorbell rings. It is precisely 12:00 noon and Diana wonders if Geoffrey has been standing outside waiting for this exact moment to ring the bell. She rushes over as her dad opens the door and grabs Geoffrey's hand as he walks in, almost presenting him to her wary parents.

'What has he done to get under Diana's skin like this?' they both wonder.

Whatever he was doing obviously worked because 4 years later, Diana and Geoffrey married in a beautiful ceremony and another 4 years after that, Diana had given birth to a beautiful little baby boy. Jacob had arrived with a huge, happy smile on his innocent little face and then proceeded to dominate their lives!

*

2022

Jake storms out of the house, slamming the door behind him and into the cool night air dialling Kenny on his smart phone as he goes. Of course, he jumps at the chance to spend the night rebel rousing with his best mate and they arrange to meet in the local park half an hour later.

'I'll bring a bottle of bourbon with me. I've got a stash under the bed that my bloody grog-soaked sponge of a father's never even missed!' Kenny brags.

They meet in the relative darkness of the park, away from the lamps along the pathways and take cover well away from prying eyes. There's nothing like the privacy of a deserted park at night and after sharing the first few gulps of the burning amber liquid, Jake feels settled enough to tell Kenny the sorry story of that night's altercation.

'He really thinks he can tell me what to do and I'll just bow and say, "Yes, Sir! No, Sir! Three bloody bags full, sir"!'

Kenny is silent for a few minutes, which is not like Kenny at all and Jake looks over at him, '*What*?'

Looking a bit embarrassed, his head hanging low, Kenny mumbles, 'At least your father cares enough to ask what you're doing. Mine's always drunk and couldn't care less.'

Jake looks quickly over at his mate. He's never heard Kenny being so candid and he certainly wasn't expecting it at that exact moment. He must really feel let down by his father to open up like that and here he was always complaining about his! He thinks he should just shut up instead of whingeing like a spoiled brat, so he tries to get back onto some sort of even level.

'Yeah but I reckon it might be better than having him in your face all the time! After tonight, I just had to get out of there!' He takes a swig and passes the bottle to Kenny.

Jake falls silent as they both sit thinking their drunken thoughts to themselves. He knows he shouldn't lump his Mum in with his dad. She does try to do the right thing by him and she did always support him with the school but the poor old thing keeps putting her foot in it. And his dad just walks all over her!

'Mum's alright, you know,' he tells Kenny, 'I shouldn't yell at *her*! But I just don't know how she can stay married to that controlling bastard for as long as she has! Sometimes I just wish he was *dead*!' Jake scowls as he takes a swig.

'Yeah, know what you mean, I feel like that too sometimes!' he stops and tries to garner his drunken thoughts, looking for more justification. 'But you've gotta *love* the way they just shove you in "the best and most prestigious school" they can find and then never let you forget what it's costing them while they congratulate themselves on what bloody great parents they are!

'And then they constantly whinged at me when I was there because I hated it! "*Do you know how much this is costing us to send you there? You could be a Doctor or a Lawyer!*" What? Do they want us to pay them back or something?

Stupid thing is I like the new public school much better anyway and it's miles cheaper so that should keep them happy.' Swig!

'Same, mate! I get the doctor and lawyer speech all the time but I don't want to be a *lawyer* or a *doctor*, so why should I bust my balls? I've seen what bein' a doctor 'as done for *my* old man! And NO thank *you*!' Swig. And then they both start laughing hysterically.

Exhausted and breathless, Kenny looks over and tries to focus on Jake but the world is getting very blurry. 'Sho what you gonna do?' Swig.

'Dunno yet, nothin' prob'ly, don't 'ave to! My dad's rollin' in it, let '*im* keep me! After all, they're the ones who wanted kids! I dint ashk to be born!' Swig. Jake shakes the bottle but it's empty. 'Ohh, it'sh all gone!' He pulls his lip down and pretends to wipe a tear away from his eye, tossing the empty bottle over behind a bush where he hears it smash against all the other discarded bottles. 'Kiddiesh can't go back there!' he slurs, waving his hand in the general direction of the mess.

'Nah!' answers the bleary Kenny.

They sit there in silence for a while before they start complaining about their lives again. The initial buzz of the bourbon has started to wear off and with no more alcohol in sight, boredom is setting in.

'So, whatta ya wanna do now?' Jake asks wondering where they could get another bottle.

'Dunno. Could steal a car or somethin'!' Kenny shrugs, laughing but as he's only half joking, there's no real mirth in the hollow sounding cackle. They've both been in trouble before and something like this would definitely put them both in the slammer. Should they risk it?

Jake jumps up excitedly spurred on by the idea and almost shouts at Kenny, '*YES!* That's *it,* you're bloody brilliant! Let's nick old Peasey's pretty noo sports car! Bastard was whingein' about me to the Olds the other day. So, *I'll show him.*'

'Yeah! Let's do it! But are you sure, mate? I mean, he's right next door to ya and everything?' Kenny's just been thinking how Jake seems to have been affected by the drink a lot more than he has tonight and surmises that he must have started early on his own dad's stuff before he came out. It could just be the drink talking, not the brain.

But with Jake already heading out through the park on his way back home to pay a little unexpected visit to "that stuck up prick next-door" fuelled by both alcohol and a burning revenge, Kenny has quite a job keeping up with him and no chance at all of talking him out of it.

When they reach the Peasey's front door, Kenny starts feeling decidedly nervous about going through with it. He tries to put Jake off by asking if they're not going to need the keys for this one. They both know it's a problem with these new cars, the only way they knew to get the job done was with the keys. Neither of them is mechanically minded and he doesn't think the old hot-wiring trick would work here anyway, even if they knew how to do it.

'Don' worry, they're hangin' on a hook just behind that little glass window there, next to the door. You smash the glass and grab the keys for me and then nickin' off in his precious sports car will be 'Easy Peasey!' He laughs out loud at his own joke, 'Get it? Easy *Peasey*?' Until Kenny shushes him so he doesn't wake the whole bloody neighbourhood!

Jake sees Kenny hesitating in front of the glass panel and roughly pushes him out of the way. 'Pussy!' he yells and smashes the glass himself, scooping the keys off their hook and hightailing it into the garage.

The sound of glass shattering and the garage door opening wakes Richard Peasey and his wife Jennifer with a start from their sound sleep. Jenny sits straight up and clutches the bedclothes to her chin in fear.

'Get them, Richard!' she whispers, afraid that the intruders are actually in the house and bizarrely thinking her virtue is the only thing that's under threat. Richard grabs a ski stock from their wardrobe, the only thing he can think of to use as a weapon and starts to tiptoe down the stairs ready to take on all comers or so he tells himself.

As he reaches the bottom landing, he hears the distinctive note of his new Porsche's engine starting and he races out the front door, stands on the front lawn and shakes his fist in the air screaming 'Stop! Thieves!' But he's too late and all he sees is his beloved little car without him in it, speeding off down the street, tyres squealing and taillights winking until it's out of sight.

'No!' he screams but there's no-one out there to hear him, so he stomps determinedly back in the door and through to the kitchen, snatching the phone up from its charging cradle on the way and calls the police.

*

35

'Sarge, we've got a stolen car,' says a young officer to his more senior partner and Sergeant. '126 Cleveland Way.' He radios back that they're on their way as the older officer executes a U-Turn and heads back the way they've just come, towards the Peasey's home. Richard is standing back out on the front lawn, keeping watch for the police to arrive and he's starting to feel the chill of the night air seeping through his pyjamas and dressing gown. Where are they?

The police have almost reached their destination when they receive another call over the radio; there's been a single vehicle car accident with casualties, can they attend? They give the address and it's very close to where they are now.

'That's just down the road, Sarge, do you want to take it?'

'Yeah, let them know. ETA is six minutes.'

They roll up to the scene of the accident to find a beautifully maintained Porsche concertinaed into the back of an unidentifiably mangled parked car. What a mess! This can't be a coincidence, so they check the number plates and sure enough, the Porsche is the missing vehicle they were just about to check on. Inside the car, they find an unconscious Kenny in the passenger seat and a groggy and very drunk Jake slumped over the wheel.

'Bloody idiots!' The older guy remarks and the constable radios for an ambulance. ASAP.

*

Half an hour later, the two officers arrive on the Peasey's doorstep.

'You lot took your time!' Richard snaps, 'they'll be in Victoria before you even start looking for them!'

'No, I'm afraid not, Sir. Actually, they only made it about three kilometres away before they met with a parked car. I'm sorry sir but it looks like your car might be a write off.'

'Great! So, what about the thieves? Did you at least get *them*? My new car's a wreck and look at the damage they did to our front door!'

'Yes, sir. We have them both. They've been taken to the hospital. The passenger's in a bad way but the driver was semi-conscious when we got to the scene. He doesn't seem to be too badly hurt but at the moment, they won't let us speak to him until he sobers up.'

'I should have guessed.' Richard throws his hands in the air in a gesture of hopeless disbelief. 'Drunk as skunks, eh? Well, thank you, officer. Can you please keep me informed? And I'll want to press charges, too!'

'Sir.'

'Right, so where's my car now?'

The older officer gives him the business card of the tow truck company who have taken his car away and then they take their farewells, promising to keep him updated.

At that exact moment, the phone starts ringing in the McMullen's lounge room.

*

Two days later, a battered and bruised Jake stands in front of the magistrate trying to look sedate and remorseful but still radiating smug self-assurance in spite of himself. After all, he's been here before and nothing really happens. This guy will just send him home with another warning, his dad will yell at him and that's usually the end of it. But something grabs his attention, what was that, what's he saying?

'Jacob McMullen. You've been charged with high level drink driving, break and enter and car theft. How do you plead?'

This is it, time to look sorry and give him my best "little lost boy" look, it works every time! But this time, he's not in the Juvenile Court having recently turned 18 and the "little lost boy" routine holds no water with the world-weary magistrate seated before him.

'Guilty, sir and sorry!' he repeats almost parroting his last two appearances. But this time to his horror, his rehearsed and "heartfelt" sorry is definitely not enough.

'Save the "sorry" for later, Mr McMullen. The defendant will be held in remand and as this is not his first offence, bail is set at $5000.' And the gavel bangs with finality on the sound block as if to say "Next?"

Jake looks quickly around to his parents, shocked that he's not just walking out and going home with them. What just happened? A guard comes up, takes him by the arm and escorts him physically out of the courtroom.

Sitting in the holding cell, he thinks about the predicament he's found himself in. $5000! Wow, that's a pretty substantial sum but he's not worried, after all that's only a pittance to his father. He's bought bottles of whisky worth more than that!

So, he guesses he'll just sit here and wait until they come and get him. It's never got this far before and he doesn't quite know exactly what to expect or how it all works, so he'll just wait.

After what seems like hours, he's taken to a bus for transport with some other guys to Mountview Prison where he'll be held until his trial. He's both confused and indignant, protesting in a slightly panicked voice that, 'No, you don't understand! I'm just waiting for my dad to pay the bail. How will he know where I am?'

'No mate, *you* don't understand. Your dad's not bailing you out this time. We hope you enjoy your stay with us,' he adds in a fake, gentrified tone and the other prisoners laugh at this stupid, naïve boy as the guard pushes Jake roughly into the vehicle.

*

'We can't just leave him there, Geoffrey,' Diana pleads still weeping and unable to believe how cold-hearted her husband is being leaving their only son to rot in jail like this.

'Sorry, Diana but a bit of time in there might be just what he needs! I'm not going to keep bailing him out of trouble just so he can go out and do it all again! And he or that Kenny, could have been killed this time! Or some innocent bystander. How would you feel if they'd crashed into a car with children in it? No, he can just wait it out and stew in his own juices. Maybe it'll give him time to think long and hard about what's he's done. I might even send in a dictionary so he can look up the words, "actions" and "consequences".'

*

When Jake arrives at the jail, he asks straight away if he can ring his mother, he knows she'll sort it all out. An almost friendly guard tells him he can as soon as all the necessary paperwork etc. has been finalised.

Ok, then. He'll do all that first.

But he quickly finds out that the paperwork is far easier than the "etc." and by the time he's dressed in the regulation prison green track suit and told to 'Wait there!' he's visibly shaken, upset and even more confused. Without his own clothes, he feels like they've stripped him of his very identity, reducing them all to the same faceless, nameless carbon copies of each other.

He's feeling more unsure and vulnerable than he ever has before and he really needs to talk to his mother; the sooner the better. The first officer he'd spoken to comes over to him with a cordless phone and stands there while he dials his home, hoping against hope that his Mum answers it and not his father.

Diana does and bursts into tears at the sound of her son's voice. She promises that she'll try to talk Geoffrey around when he calms down so just try to be patient. He feels a bit of comfort at that; at least one of them is on his side and telling her that he hopes he can talk to her again soon, he ends the call, hands the phone back to the waiting guard and bursts into tears.

*

Back in her home, Diana looks down at the silent phone and knows that she just has to try as hard as she can to get Geoffrey to pay the bail, she has no other option and she wishes with all her being that she had put some money aside of her own but she hasn't.

One thing she knows for sure is that she cannot leave her boy in there all alone. She tries to frame in her mind how she's going to approach Geoffrey, how she's going to try to make him listen for a change. But she knows too well that he can be as immovable as a rock when his mind's made up and deep down, she knows that keeping her promise to Jacob is definitely going to be a lot easier said than done!

Chapter Three
2022-Mountview Prison

'Right, come on mate.' Jake looks up and wonders what's next for him and where he's going now as he stands nervously. The guard takes his arm, escorting him to his cell and stands at the door, barking instructions to him about mealtimes, making his bed and where he *can* go on the premises as opposed to what's out of bounds.

Jake's mind is spinning. He's finding it very hard to take in everything the guard's saying to him, actually he's finding it hard to take in anything that's happening to him at all! 'So, I don't have to stay in here all day then?' Jake asks and the guard looks him up and down.

'Huh, another newbie. He'll learn,' he thinks but relaxing his tone to one of a concerned uncle says, 'this is only one step up from minimum security, son. You can go into the yard, the TV room and the meals area. But that's it, OK?'

'Thank you, Sir.' Jake nods, his face still a mask of uncertainty, his usual colour drained by fear. He feels himself taken back to that first day he was in trouble at school. He can remember clearly sitting in Mr Sanderson's office and feeling just as uncertain and nervous as he's feeling right now but at least he had his Mum beside him back then and he remembers feeling the warm protection of her loving presence. This time however he's on his own.

'Look, it's almost dinner time. Why don't you leave your things in here and head down now? Might break the ice for ya a bit.' And with that he stalks off, leaving Jake to himself. He looks around the tiny cell, taking everything in and wondering how on earth he's going to survive in this place.

The other bed doesn't even look like it's being slept in; maybe he has the room to himself, he thinks hopefully. The bed has been made with what looks like military precision, so someone's done that but there are no personal items around, no pictures on the wall or belongings on the bedside table.

He wonders what became of the other guy. Did he go home or did he go the other way to a real prison? This place seems to be a bit of a waiting room until the court decides your future. No wonder it looks so empty and unlived in.

'What did you expect, the days crossed off on the wall or something?' he asks himself and taking a last look around the cell, he ventures out.

*

When he returns an hour and a half later, his hopes of having the room to himself are dashed. Another young guy, maybe in his early to mid-twenties, is sitting on the other bed reading and he looks up smiling at the sight of Jake almost tip-toeing in.

'G'day.'

Jake nods and heads over to his bed.

They proceed to give each other a wary once over, first impressions already formed and expectations already set. Jake thinks, '*Geek*!' while the other guy looks up at him thinking, '*Poor kid.*'

He's also wearing the uniform prison greens and has a pair of wire-framed spectacles perched precariously on the edge of his nose, which causes him to lift his chin and look down his nose to be able to focus on his new cellmate.

Jake, however, interprets this as an arrogant sense of ownership; a marking of his territory and wonders exactly what Geek Boy has made of him but then straight away decides that it doesn't matter in the least because neither of them are probably going to be here for long and he doesn't really care anyway!

As he crashes down on his bed, flat on his back and hands behind his head in what he hopes is a confident, nothing new here attitude, the door suddenly swings shut behind him, the electronic lock slamming into place and Jake realises that this is it. He's really in *jail*.

He's really locked in until morning and with a total stranger to boot. He can feel his nerves and his false bravado starting to crumble.

The other guy smiles at the surprise on Jake's face and pushing the loose spectacles back up his nose, says, 'Hi! I'm Danny!' He reaches his hand out to shake Jake's but Jake totally ignores the gesture, instead grunting what he thinks is a prison-tough greeting and looks away.

'And you are?'

'Jake.'

'Well, Jake, you just made that in the nick of time! Didn't you hear the alarm?'

The last thing he needs right now is a chatty cellmate, he just wants to be left alone to wallow in his own misery. He mumbles something about hearing an alarm but not knowing what it was for, so Danny fills him in on a few things that will definitely be in his best interest to keep in mind from now on, finishing with 'So, where are you from?'

'Sydney.'

'Me too, now,' he answers, although Jake never asked the question. 'But you can probably tell by my accent I'm from the UK originally.'

'So how did you end up in Australia then?' He smirks as if he's caught Danny out in a lie. UK my foot, he thinks, that accent might be straight from Liverpool alright but it's from Liverpool, New South Wales, *not* Liverpool, England. Danny was from nowhere near the teeming docks of the Mersey.

'My parents own land in Hertfordshire and decided that coming here for a year to work on an Australian farm would be a good experience for me and would teach me a bit more about farming and agriculture.' He shrugs, 'you can see for yourself how that worked out.'

He pauses remembering. 'You know, I wasn't happy about coming over here at all. I really didn't want to leave all my mates behind and why here? Could they find any place further away? But as it turned out, I actually enjoyed working on the farm, the other blokes who worked there were great too.'

Jake lets him rave on, not sure what would happen if he tried to stop him anyway and despite himself, he starts getting involved in his story.

*

Danny

Danny jumps down from Cheryl's car after the long, dusty drive from Dubbo airport and stands hesitantly, not knowing what to expect. He's hot, thirsty and wishes he'd brought more sensible clothes for this stifling climate than these silly tweeds.

The boys each grab a hand and pull him eagerly along to where Mr and Mrs Robertson are standing, shielding their eyes from the harsh sun. He walks up and holds out his hand for Mr Robertson to shake but Mrs Robertson just throws her arms around him in a warm and welcoming hug and he's soon feeling like he's a part of the family and relaxes into it easily.

Cheryl takes a proprietary interest in him, having picked him up from the airport and appoints herself his "Tour Guide and Entertainment Co-ordinator", which he doesn't object to in the least!

Mrs Robertson has made a delicious roast lamb dinner with all the trimmings to "make him feel at home" and they spend the night sitting on the veranda talking and learning more about each other, until they all realise what time it is and turn in for the night.

He's learned that the work days start at daybreak on this farm and as he gets ready for bed, he can't help wondering what they have for breakfast down here. He thinks about his home with their sideboard filled to overflowing with kippers, eggs, bacon, sausages and a steaming bowl of porridge from eight o'clock on. Anything earlier than that would be unthinkable and uncivilised. So, starting work at daybreak is a real culture shock.

Accordingly, the next morning the alarm wakes him at dawn and he realises that it's his first full day at Whitegum. He sits on the veranda, drinking his tea and looking in awe at the pink cirrus clouds scattered across the morning sky.

Last night's sunset had been the most spectacular thing he'd ever seen, the turquoise sky meeting the orange horizon with the promise of a hot and sunny day to follow. And then as the sky had slowly turned a deep navy blue, thousands of tiny stars appeared.

They were quite muted around the almost full moon, which flooded the sky with a soft white light casting the gumtrees and outhouses into stark black silhouettes but they shone brightly the further away from the moon you moved, illuminating the deep, eternal darkness beyond.

He'd never seen anything like this before and he sat with Cheryl on the veranda steps, looking skyward as she pointed out some of the famous southern hemisphere constellations, including the Southern Cross. He'd already made his mind up that he was definitely going to like this outdoors style of living and is equally looking forward to starting work the next day and as Mr Robertson would say, getting his hands dirty.

The morning's peace is broken as workers start piling in from their respective homesteads, which are sprinkled across the thousands of acres of the property and that's also something he has trouble getting his head around. He'll have to work it out later but he's convinced this farm might be about as big as England and Wales combined!

Unbelievable. He is introduced to the men as "an apprentice from England, here to learn how we do it down here". To a man they all smirk, taking in his white legs and fair complexion and think the same thing; he'll never make it, if the hard work doesn't get him, the flies and the sunburn will!

But Danny confounds them all. He gets stuck into whatever they throw his way for the rest of the week and come Friday, he's earned their grudging respect.

'Comin' for a beer?' asks the foreman. It's the last thing he feels like doing, he doesn't even drink that much really but he doesn't want to throw his hospitality back in his face and lose what little ground he's made through the rest of the week.

'And what? I'm not invited?' comes a mischievous voice from the back of the shed. Cheryl's standing there wiping sweat from her brow with a bandana and wearing her signature face-splitting smile.

'Course y'are, luv! See yas down in the Sheaf later on then.'

The "Golden Sheaf" is the local that all the men are drawn to like magnets every Friday night after work and this week is no exception. They all have a raucous night and by the end of it, Danny has been introduced to so many people in Narromine that he knows he has no hope of ever remembering them all! So, he just stays close to Cheryl the whole time and keeps smiling and nodding.

When he comes to early the next morning, he has the worst headache he thinks he's ever had. His mouth is dry and tastes foul and it takes him a while to realise that this is a hangover; his first hangover and he decides then and there, it will also be his last.

He works harder than ever all day, guzzling water constantly and then losing it just as quickly through the pores of his skin. His shirt and singlet are saturated, due to the stinking hot sun under which he's been relentlessly hammering fence posts and tying red hot wire.

Cheryl is worried about him. The other men are used to these harsh working conditions but Danny is so wiry and pale, she keeps thinking that he might pass out. She's tried to get him to come in for lunch at least to cool down a bit but he just says he's not going to let his stupidity of last night affect his work today. And after a while, she gives up.

He keeps to his word and after that, he always declines the offer of beers on a Friday night, preferring to sit on the veranda talking about the history of the

*

'What about you? Have you always lived in Sydney?' Danny asks as he finishes giving Jake a brief rundown of his life.

'Yeah, grew up here. But I haven't worked anywhere yet, not like you. I'm still at school; year 12 but not for much longer now.' He adds dejectedly, 'When they hear about this, they'll chuck me out for sure!'

He wonders if Danny's story was real or not, 'If not, I bet he'd like it to be!' he thinks. But one thing he does know for sure is it has made him feel like a bit of a loser and he doesn't know what he can do about that. He feels a bit ticked off that he would tell him that story to point out his own weaknesses, so he goes back to trying hard with his adopted tough-guy nonchalance to show Danny that it hadn't worked.

His confidence is intact. But in truth, he knows he's hiding the real disappointment he feels at the thought that he might not sit for his Higher School Certificate. He's always felt that he has to make out he doesn't care and doesn't need it but deep down, he knows that's not true. Guess what is true is that he's just a loser.

Danny's not taken in with his "tough-guy, I-don't-give-a-damn" act, picking up on the casual way Jake referred to being "chucked out" of school but at the same time seeing how his face belied that sentiment and he firmly believes that Jake is not being truthful about his feelings, not even to himself.

He can see by his expression that Jake feels like he's blown his chance at finishing year 12 and in a way that might spur him on to do better when he gets out of here. But he can't help wondering if Jake has actually thought past the exam and the formal.

He's often thought that sitting the HSC is seen by too many students as the end of the story when it's really just the beginning of the rest of their lives. And having to finish school this way will probably have a far greater impact on the rest of this young guy's life than he seems to realise right now.

Whenever this happens to young kids like this, they all know a conviction will be on their record forever and will come against them when they're trying to get a job. But what they don't think about is that the lack of education itself, along with the missing qualifications, can do just as much damage.

'So, you really don't care if you get expelled? Is that what you're saying?'

Danny's question is met with another shrug and a grunt of, 'Not the first time. Nah, I don't care,' from Jake who is still looking sulky, resentful and incredibly sorry for himself. A pregnant pause stretches into an awkward silence as if Danny's just waiting for Jake to fill it.

But Jake doesn't meet his eyes, instead focusing on one very clear thought that's been running through his mind since Danny began *his* story. 'If he thinks I'm going to give him the whole sorry story of *my* life, then he has another think coming.' And that is written so clearly all over his closed face that Danny can almost hear the next line, "End of conversation!"

But instead of leaving him to wallow in his own misery, he becomes even more determined to get this guy talking. Sulking won't help anything for Jake and Danny's not going to spend his time in here with all this self-absorbed rubbish going on day after day either.

So, he takes a deep breath realising that *Jake* might believe he's closed up shop for the night but he's in for a big shock because he's not finished with him yet, not by a long shot. He's also getting thoroughly sick of all the rude and dismissive replies, so he ploughs right in.

'Well, young Jake,' he says in his soothing, well-bred English accent, 'Let me tell you something for nothing. Your time in here will go a lot more smoothly if you just take it easy and try to get along. It doesn't matter how tough you think you are on the outside, just remember there'll always be someone tougher in here and believe me, you won't want to go making waves!'

Jake looks up quickly, was that a threat? But looking into Danny's eyes, he feels anything but threatened so he apologises and explains briefly, 'First time. Don't know what I'm supposed to be doing!'

Danny just nods his understanding and says, 'Don't worry, you'll be right!' Silence reigns until Danny asks, trying to keep his voice light and interested, 'OK, so what did you do to find yourself banged up in here?'

Jake looks over at Danny and smiles for the first time. This is his first chance to show Geek Boy he's not just a random kid who got caught stealing lollies! He's the genuine article. Set the ground rules, he thinks, that's the way to do it. And I'll be the one setting all the rules while I'm here with this geek! Start off as you intend to carry on, someone had once told him.

So, he puffs his chest up and tells Danny just what he wants him to hear to get some respect.

'You should have seen it!' he laughs, 'I had a bit of a big night out with my mate, Kenny!' he brags, 'and we drank a *whole bottle* of bourbon between us but I'd started earlier when I got into some of Dad's precious *Good* whisky and then I thought, "This might just be the prime time to get even with that stuck up prick next-door. Richard *Peasey*, can you believe? *Easy* Peasey, more like it"!'

He goes on bragging as if he needs to validate what he did, the child again pleading his case with an angry mother. 'Bastard's been badmouthing me to my 'Olds' and they just stood there agreeing with him! Some parents, eh? So, I got *him* back and gave Mum and Dad a night *they'll* never forget at the same time.'

'What, by getting drunk?' Danny looks totally unconvinced and thoroughly unimpressed. This kid's been watching too much television, he thinks. He looks at Jake and takes note of his pose and his attitude. He can see that Jake has cultivated this look, probably from some on-screen hero or other and he obviously thinks this is what's expected of him in here! He shakes his head.

'No. Not *just* by getting drunk! That part was only the warmup to the main event. See, Peasey had just bought himself a *cute little* Porsche what, about two weeks ago so I thought I'd take it for a spin, didn't I?' he cackles triumphantly. 'Had to smash the glass in the front door to get the keys and that was a bummer 'cause it woke them up and I didn't get the head start I wanted.

'But then it worked out better 'cause he ran out of the house screaming like a mad man. We broke up laughing when we saw his face, old man Peasey, I mean. There he was, standing on the lawn in his pyjamas; smoke blowing out of his ears and shaking his fist in the air.'

He laughs and waits for a response but getting none decides to go on with the story. 'So, we just waved him goodbye and he didn't see *us* for *dust*! I tell ya, I was so glad I'd seen that. I just wish I could have seen Mum and Dad's faces too when they realised it was *me* who did it. Their *little* baby *boy*!'

He's virtually crowing with delight that he's had such a fabulous story to share. Now he'll know that he's not someone to mess with! He's got real form! Of course, he has no idea what "real form" means. He's just seen it on the telly and thought it was something he really should have if he wanted to be taken seriously.

Danny, however, had read something entirely different in Jake's story. He's not a bad kid just on the wrong track, obviously spoiled but nevertheless desperately unhappy. He'd get to that later but right now, he had noticed the healing injuries on Jake's arms and legs, you could hardly miss them and sees clearly that the whole thing could not possibly have gone as "successfully" as Jake would like him to believe.

And regardless of Jake's excitement and justifications, he's definitely not impressed with what they did. Jake's treating it all as a silly practical joke gone wrong but from what he's just described, he's in serious trouble.

'So, how'd you end up with all the cuts and bruises, then?'

'Pranged the bloody car, didn't I? It was a write off but in a way, it was a poetic end to the night.'

'Poetic? Strange word to use! And by the way, what happened to Kenny? Do you even care?' Danny asks, noticing that he's been conspicuously absent from the narrative. It was like Jake wanted to take all the "credit" for himself.

Jake answers, instantly more subdued, that he doesn't really know what's happened to him. He hasn't been able to see him or talk to him since he left the hospital that night but Kenny was still unconscious then and they'd kept him in. Since then, they won't tell him anything.

His Mum's going to try to find out how he's getting on and also what the doctors are saying. Danny can see he's extremely upset, so much so that he totally forgets about keeping up his tough guy act and momentarily lets his real self peek through.

'Let's hope, for your sake as well as Kenny's, that he is OK. Hope it was all worth it!' He pauses to let that start to sink in. 'OK now tell me, why you really did it? And don't just say it was because he complained about you to your parents!'

'No, not just *one* complaint! Bagging me is what he lives for! And I'm sick of it. I just wanted revenge. I thought to myself "If that's what they think I am then that's what I'll be. I'll show them. I'll show them *all*." And I did!'

Danny makes a point of looking around the room, gesturing with his hand as if to say welcome to your new home and just says, 'Yeah, I guess you did. But just *what* did you show them?'

Jake feels like he's been slapped across the face. He thought the people in here would be like-minded and would be able to see how clever he'd been. Although he has to admit, maybe not so clever in the end if anything bad has happened to Kenny or they both end up in jail for years.

But he soon shakes that off as he realises that Danny was actually just having a go at him! Just like everybody else! He turns angrily to him, 'Not you too?'

'Yep, me too. You've got to start doing some serious thinking, mate. Being in here is not about your neighbours or your parents or what I think. It's only about you; "Jacob". You need to work out what made you so angry that you ended up doing something that landed you in here in the first place.'

Jake rolls his eyes, 'A bloody do-gooder!' And how did he know his name was "Jacob"? He only said he was Jake!

'Yeah, well, they all *bug* me! I just wanted to prove to them that I could get them back, that's all.' His voice has taken on the sulky tone of a child again. 'And besides, I didn't think they'd throw me in *here* this time! Or that my own father would *leave* me here!

'He won't even pay the bail. Justice, they call it; don't make me laugh. *Injustice* more like it; that's all I've ever got in here and back at home as well! Same old story. I mean it's not as if I'm a *murderer* or anything, am I?' He pauses and throws Danny a cautious glance through narrowed eyes; *he's* not, *is he*?

But Danny doesn't seem to notice Jake's hesitation, he's too busy thinking, 'This time. So, it's not the first time he's been in trouble, eh? OK.'

He turns to look Jake straight in the eyes. 'Mate, you don't know how lucky you've been or how good you've had it. I reckon you've been a bit of a mug myself. So, come on, tell me what really brought it all on? It's not normal for a boy your age to be so angry over such a stupid little thing.'

'Don't start with that "my age" crap. You sound just like *them*. I'm *eighteen;* a man now and I'm sick to death of being treated like a kid. Do you know what? If I do something they don't *approve* of, they still think they can punish me like I *am* still a kid!

'Can you believe they put me on a ten o'clock curfew just because I stayed out all night? Bloody ridiculous! When are they ever going to realise that I'm a grown man and treat me like an adult?'

Maybe when you start acting like one and keep out of trouble. He answers himself and frowns; where did *that* come from?

'Mm, so now you're here. *Permanent* curfew. Like it or lump it. *And* complaining about justice? How do you think Mr Peasey feels about justice? He worked all his life and saved hard for that car and you not only just waltzed in and helped yourself to it but you destroyed it as well. And yet you think you're the one that's hard done by.'

'Of course, I'm hard done by. I'm *here*, aren't I?'

'You are and you don't even know how good you've got it in here either. These days you're treated like a real person in jail. You're kept warm and dry and fed, you've got television and clean clothes. You should have seen how bad it was in the old days! You've got no idea.'

What the—? This guy really is a bit strange. Maybe he's a teacher or something, yeah, he's got that look. Jake doesn't see how the conditions back then can either affect or help him now! And he certainly doesn't need any more lectures, he's starting to get bored.

'So? What's that got to do with me?' he asks belligerently. He watches as Danny stops, pushes his glasses back up his nose and takes a deep breath.

'Do you *really* want to know? Because I can definitely show you!'

'Go on then, may as well. No telly in here anyway. All right then, you think you're so smart, tell me about these bad old days!'

'Oh, you want an example, do you? Righto, let me think, justice. OK, here's the perfect example of medieval justice. Now, if anybody wanted to complain about how "justice" was dished up back then and how bad she had it, Ann Boleyn would have been the one.'

'Anne who?'

'She was the second wife of King Henry VIII and she was only twenty-six when she married him, so not much older than you are now in the scheme of things.' He shakes his head slightly at the thought, 'And she was such a beautiful, young woman too!'

Jake looks at him with barely concealed frustration. Some stupid old woman back in the dark ages has got nothing to do with him being in jail now!

'So what?'

'So, *this*!' Danny starts talking, his voice smooth, calming and melodic and Jake soon finds himself being lulled into a trance-like state with images of the Tudors taking shape in his mind and as he slowly drifts away; his eyes close.

Chapter Four
1536-London, England

In an instant, garbled noises and atrocious odours, all of which are well out of place in a small jail cell in suburban Sydney, bombard his senses. Shouting voices, neighing horses and creaking carts are one thing but the overwhelming smell, both obnoxious and saturating, is the thing that triggers an immediate gag response.

He opens his eyes and slowly looks around, his mouth dropping open in shock and his eyes wide in astonishment as he stands, staring in disbelief at the sight before him. 'Where are we? Danny! What's going on? And *what's* that *smell*?' He feels shaky and panic stricken.

'This is Tudor London under the rule of King Henry VIII and the date is 18 May 1536,' Danny explains quietly. Jake looks at him and can't believe the calm, rational response. He wouldn't have been surprised to hear Danny add, "Of course!"

Danny knows only too well that Ann Boleyn's execution is scheduled for the next day. But Jake knows nothing of this, he's never been an enthusiastic reader and was an even less interested history student and he's looking around at the filthy streets and putrid state of England's biggest city of the day in awe.

People are rushing to and fro and there's an excited air to their scuttling and bustling, which reminds Jake of trips to the Sydney's Royal Easter Show when he was just little.

He turns to Danny who is standing beside him, looking grim but calm, for the answers to his questions.

'You wanted to learn about justice and this is London, 1536. Tomorrow's the day that Ann Boleyn will face the rather individual style of justice of her husband, King Henry VIII,' Danny tells him informatively.

Jake is at a loss and has no idea what Danny is talking about. He's sure they didn't learn about Henry VIII at school, so he's completely in the dark as to what "justice" Danny is actually referring to but he doesn't want to show his ignorance by asking.

'Right, so how did we get here?' he asks instead as he turns away and heaves.

'Don't worry about that now, just take it all in and we'll talk more about it when we get back.'

Danny starts walking through the tangle of bodies and carts. Jake finds it slow-going and has to push himself to keep up, mainly because he has to keep stopping along the way in violent and physical response to the stomach-churning locale.

He's never had what you might call a weak stomach but the sights and smells surrounding him have really got the better of him and he can only make it a few paces at a time without grabbing his stomach and heaving his heart out.

He can't find a way to escape the stench and covers his nose with his hand to try to block it out but all that does is attract the attention of the many people on the street, who frown threateningly at him with some actually spitting on him!

'What was *that* for?'

'They don't like outsiders and you're not exactly trying to fit in like that! Come on! We've got to find somewhere to spend the night.' They walk on through the streets with Jake pointing out various hotels and boarding houses along the way, until they finally come across a laneway which seems quieter and will give them a bit more privacy as it's tucked away from the main thoroughfare. Jake looks around and sees nothing that might suggest accommodation.

'Why are we stopping here? Where's the hotel?'

'God, you've had a sheltered upbringing, Jake! Just think of this as a one-night only camping holiday. The ground is our hotel and the sky above will have to be our blankets!'

'Are you mad? I can't sleep in all that filth! Is it even safe?'

'Probably not, that's why we'll have to take it in turns that is if we can sleep at all!'

Jake looks up at Danny, gobsmacked by the sudden comprehension of what he'd just said. He'd actually meant he was worried about the germs on the ground but Danny had made him understand now that they'll probably be pretty easy targets for all kinds of creeping thieves and thugs.

He doesn't know what Danny thinks *he* could do against people like that. He might have been a bit of a bully at his old school with Kenny beside him but he knows he'll be no match for any of these guys. He's pretty sure he's not going to get any sleep tonight, that's for sure.

And what about the police? Will they think they're just as bad if they see them sleeping here like this? He hasn't got a good feeling about any of it at all.

'But what about the police? Will we get arrested again for loitering or something?' he asks tentatively. He only half wants an answer.

Danny squats down on his haunches and tells him that there *is* no organised police force as such, just occasional members of the watch and people sleeping in the streets is not in the least unusual. Jake can't believe it. No police? But who keeps the peace in this godawful city?

Here he was worried about them getting arrested and now all he wishes for is a good old London Bobby to come along, rock on his feet, swing his baton and look after them.

But he guesses they'll just have to watch out for themselves. What Danny hasn't told Jake is that all kinds of thieves and murderers are rife in London at this time, almost a probability more than just a possibility and they totally rule the streets. Compared to what they're used to, the level of lawlessness is unimaginable so they will have to be very, *very* careful indeed!

With nothing presenting itself as dinner, they sit talking until way past midnight. The smells and sounds make sure that neither of them get any sleep anyway and Jake can't shake the violent nausea he's been suffering since they'd arrived.

As dawn breaks, they stand up, stomping their feet and rubbing their arms to warm up. Everything that can freeze has and Jake can't feel his hands or his feet. He's never even felt this cold up in the mountains where his family goes skiing every year! This chill seems to have seeped right into his bones and set up home there.

They can hear the early morning bustle of stall keepers and other workers beginning their day and Jake would love to buy something for breakfast from any one of the food vendors but they don't have any money, so Danny says that moving will warm them up as well as taking their minds off their bellies.

As soon as they leave the confines of the tiny laneway, Jake is once again assaulted full force by the state of the streets. In that moment, he feels grateful not to have eaten anything; that way he doesn't have anything left inside to lose!

'Where are we going?' God, he sounds like a kid in a car! Are we there yet?

'I want to try to get a good spot inside the Tower walls.'

So, head down, Jake hustles along trying to keep up with Danny as they push their way through the gathering hoards. Danny gives him a brief rundown of the history and circumstances leading up to today, mainly in order to take Jake's attention off his stomach!

'The King has found out that his wife, Anne, has been having an affair. He considers this betrayal as the worst kind of treason!' He snorts derisively. 'You think *you* were treated badly in our court system; well, she has just been treated like dirt under their feet and convicted outright, no real trial at all, let alone a fair one!'

'Well, why are all these people looking so excited and happy? Do they think she committed treason too?'

'After a fashion. All these people you see in the streets don't support her in any way, shape or form. They look down on her and think of her as a "whore" who thoroughly deserves what she's about to get. How dare she do this to their "beloved" King?'

Jake thinks about "what she's about to get" for a second in silence and decides they must be going to flog her! They wouldn't hit a woman, surely! He certainly hopes not; he doesn't want to see that and why should he have to? He gets the message loud and clear; he should be thankful he hasn't been beaten, just thrown in a nice, comfy jail cell. Stop being such a sissy! But just to be sure.

'So, what is she about to get?'

'You'll see.'

Jake's having a lot of trouble walking along this filthy street with piles of slippery mud and who knows what else continually blocking their way and he just wants to go back to their nice, safe cell. Who is this guy? How did they get there? Will they *ever* be able to get back?

He's worried, scared, sick and nearly suffocating in these toxic odours. He needs some fresh air! But Danny seems impervious to it all and Jake revises his first assessment of him, not a teacher but maybe a doctor? They're the only ones he can think of who are used to all these sorts of bad smells.

'Don't these people ever have a bath or at least a wash?' Jake asks, trying desperately not to breathe in as he speaks.

'No water for that!' Danny says as he points out people lying in doorways and up alleys, desperately ill. 'See all those people? They've more than likely got typhoid. Or dysentery. Or cholera! The council here tried digging wells around the city to collect the rainwater for drinking and they did do that but with no way of monitoring the safety of the water, disease just thrives.

'Probably all these poor souls lying in the street will die. And they'll more than likely die alone too because none of their families are game enough to go anywhere near them. They can't afford to have them in their houses in case they infect everyone else in the family as well.'

Jake is lost for words and silently looks at one boy in particular, probably around his age, lying in the nearest doorway while at the same time, scanning the streets collecting snapshots in his mind to analyse at a later date. After a while, he grabs Danny's arm, 'How much further now?'

'Not far. We're going to the Tower Green and watch out, here comes a dung cart!'

'A *what*?' Just when he'd thought the assault on his nostrils couldn't get any worse, a dung cart comes up level with them and the smell nearly knocks him off his already unstable feet!

'It goes around from street to street trying to collect all the animal and human waste it can but as you can see and smell, it's obviously not working too well! Aah well, at least they're trying!'

*

They arrive at the Tower and claim a spot, just inside the walls. Jake looks at the scene unfolding right in front of him.

In the centre of a grand looking quadrangle, he sees a small stage-type structure. Several official looking men are milling around, either on it or directly in front of it. He watches them while trying to work out what it all means, maybe they *are* going to beat her after all to publicly humiliate her! He starts to feel extremely squeamish *again* at the thought of this. Oh, God!

'Why couldn't they just get a divorce?' he asks Danny. 'It's only adultery!'

'Only adultery? It's definitely not *only* adultery when he's the King and she was his Queen!'

Jake looks like he's been hit by lightning. Of course, she's the Queen! Danny did say she was married to him but he hadn't put two and two together! He knows he's being an idiot but somehow doing this to the Queen only makes it ten times worse. He's absolutely flabbergasted.

'She's the *Queen*? And they're doing *this* to her?'

The crowd, however, obviously share none of his feelings as they start growing restless and the calls and jeers are deafening. If he didn't know better, he'd say they were at a football match, waiting for their favourite team to wipe the field with the opposition!

They share that same happy, anticipatory and well, almost festive mood that they would at any football match. Jake can't see any sign of sympathy or compassion on show for the young Queen at all.

Danny tells him that's because the people never wanted her as their Queen in the first place. Their loyalties are all still with the Queen Catherine of Aragon, even though she had died the January before.

'The people all think that young Anne caught the King's eye and manipulated him to get what she wanted. And that only made them love Queen Catherine even more!'

'And did Anne actually do that?'

'Well, put it this way. She did get her man and she did marry him promising a male heir, which is something the King is desperate for. But she didn't fulfil that promise, instead having a daughter, Elizabeth, although there were some reports of a tragic miscarriage on the day of Queen Catherine's funeral. So now, he just wants rid of her.'

RID? Jake spins around to question Danny about what that means exactly when a commotion starts in the crowd around him.

He follows their pointing fingers and angry retorts but all he can see is an extremely beautiful young woman being led to the steps of the "stage". She is wearing a dark grey cloak with some sort of fur decoration and a white bonnet and she walks up the steps with enormous dignity.

He watches as she hands something to a man wearing a hood and has a few private words with him. She takes off her cloak to show a long, slender neck and the crowd gasps as she turns towards them and they get a clear view of a splash of red beneath her gown.

She starts praying and then a curious thing happens. The crowd who'd been braying for her blood a few moments before falls silent and a lot of the onlookers stand and start praying with her through their tears. So, Jake thinks, some of them do have hearts after all.

She starts speaking of the charges against her and refuses to accuse anybody else of any wrongdoing at all for what is about to take place. Instead, she praises the King as a kind and gentle man and prays for his long reign over them all.

She then kneels down to accept her fate and Jake is so intent on watching her face, he doesn't see the razor-sharp sword being lifted into the air and then in the blink of an eye, the hooded executioner does his job.

And Jake faints.

Chapter Five
2022-Mountview

When he comes around, Danny's words, 'Don't worry, I've got you!' are still ringing in his ears. He's lying on the floor of their cell, dazed and confused, his heart pounding and his mouth dry.

'What just happened then?' he asks a concerned Danny. 'How did we get back here?'

Danny helps him up and onto his bed, where he sits with him and argues in his mind whether to call a guard or not. He wasn't expecting him to black out like that!

'Back here? Mate, we didn't go anywhere! We're in a locked cell in case you've forgotten!' Danny pushes his glasses back up his nose and clears his throat. 'And I'm not sure what happened. I was giving you a bit of a history lesson on justice and when I got to the end of Anne Boleyn's story, you just keeled over!'

Jake starts shaking all over as what he'd witnessed comes flashing back to him in graphic detail. The whole experience has made him feel physically ill from the beginning to the end. He could still smell those foul streets and the suffocating stench of collective unwashed bodies crowding him in.

He starts to feel a bit light-headed and takes a huge gulp of the fresh, filtered prison air. As his breathing settles, he looks at Danny and shakes his head. 'No! No! I don't buy it. I don't know how you did it but I *know* we were there!'

'Sorry mate, I just thought it might help if you knew what punishment was like back then to how it is today. You're so sure you've been dealt a bum deal, both being in here and also back at home with your curfews and everything. Sorry.'

Jake starts thinking about his tough guy stand on the injustice of everything that's happened to him and starts to feel more than a bit foolish. He did, after all, commit the crimes he's been charged with; guilty as charged, sir! And yet he thought he should just go home with his parents? What an idiot!

'I suppose if you look at what I did, I shouldn't have expected any less,' he starts slowly, trying to verbalise his evolving ideas. 'It's not like they're going to kill me for it, are they? Not like they killed her just for having an affair. God, these days if you murdered someone for that, you'd get a life sentence yourself. But just because he was the King, he thought he could do whatever he wanted and he got away with it by saying it was "justice".'

'You're right, there was no justice in that punishment for that crime.'

Danny looks at Jake and thinks, 'So, he's got the brains! Too bad he didn't use them!' but just says, 'Exactly. And don't forget, even though you're in here, you've got it pretty good! Just imagine what going to jail would have been like back then.' He shudders, 'Think about *that* when you're having your next nice hot shower and sitting down to three meals a day *every* day!'

'Yeah, and if I *ever* get out of here,' he says mournfully, which makes Danny smile, 'I'll never knock my curfew again, I promise!'

'Good. But?' Danny is sensing there are still unanswered questions and wonders what's going through Jake's mind now. 'Look, I know you were really shocked that she was executed, weren't you? Even though you were looking right at the gallows.'

'Yeah, I really didn't expect that. I didn't even think it was a gallows. I just thought it was some kind of stage so everyone could see.'

'See what? What *did* you think was going to happen?'

Jake tells Danny that he thought they were going to humiliate her by beating her publicly and he was dreading seeing *that* enough! But never in a million years did he think something so brutal and savage, was about to happen. At the very thought of it, he feels the squeamish tumult in his tummy starting to erupt again and he just wants to lie down.

How is he ever going to rid himself of those scenes? He closes his eyes and flashbacks are being projected onto the inside of his eyelids. Anne walking up the steps, Anne speaking to the hooded man, Anne undoing the tie on her cloak and—suddenly he sits bolt upright.

'There *was* something else I was going to ask you. When she took the cape off and turned around, everybody sort of gasped and pointed at her dress. She had something red on, is that what they were pointing at? And what was wrong with it anyway?'

'Nothing was really wrong with it. It's just that back in those times colours used to mean different things. To most of those people, red was the colour of martyrs, so I guess that's how they saw it. But it was also prescribed by doctors, would you believe? They thought certain colours against your skin could ward off "bad humours" as they called them and red was the colour they prescribed to make you feel better, so maybe she just needed that extra bit of comfort at the end.'

'That's sad.' Jake feels for her, even though he obviously never knew her.

'It is and just an extra bit of trivia for you, the red bit you saw was actually her kirtle.'

'Did you say kirtle or girdle?' Jake's heard his mother talking about wearing girdles in the old days but he doesn't think he's ever heard of a kirtle before.

'No, kirtle. It was a kind of petticoat or tunic they wore under their dresses and red was a popular colour for those things as well. So, it probably wasn't as unexpected as they all seemed to think.'

Jake is quiet, thinking about her needing her red kirtle for comfort at a time like that, just like he used to need his teddy and Chelsea needed her blanket. But obviously never for anything so drastic. And it struck him that he was very pleased those people had stood and prayed with her. He just hopes she saw it too.

Danny's watching him sitting quietly, lost in thought.

'Looks like you've taken a lot out of this story, Jake. You know, if you can keep hold of those thoughts about how unbalanced justice can be in the wrong hands, it'll really help you in the future to make fair and reasonable choices yourself and to be the best *Dad* you can be when your time comes, too!'

'*Dad*?' Jake laughs, 'Give me a break!'

'Don't worry the time will come sooner than you think, that's just the nature of time; as they say, it flies.' Danny starts stripping off his track suit to hop into bed and Jake follows suit. He vaguely wonders if all the other prisoners do that too or do they wear their trackies to bed like pyjamas?

But then decides that it really doesn't matter because nobody can see what they're doing in here anyway. Somehow that doesn't feel as comforting as it should. He's about to go to sleep in a locked room with a total stranger. But there's nothing he can do about that now.

Still, he doesn't feel sleepy at all and he knows it'll take him a long time to drop off tonight and by then, Danny will probably be sound asleep anyway.

'I don't know how I'll be able to sleep tonight after that. I can't get it out of my mind!'

'Here.' Danny hands him a leather-bound book and a pen.

'What's this?' Jake asks, flicking through the blank pages, frowning. 'A blank book?'

'It's not a book, it's a diary! The best way to clear your mind is to write everything down while it's all fresh in your memory!'

'OK, thanks!' May as well give it a go, he thinks, nothing else to do anyway.

He opens it up to the first page and starts to write.

'Do I have to write "Dear Diary"?'

'You can write anything you want. You're the only one that's ever going to read it.' And with that, Danny takes out his library book, puts his head down and starts reading, leaving Jake in relative peace.

*

Dear Diary,

Day One, Monday.

This is going to be a doozy of a first entry. What a day!

First of all, I'm not home tonight, where I thought I'd be; I'm in *jail*! I feel like I've been put through the wringer and I hate to say it but I really miss home. Even Chelsea! I wish I could fill her in on what just happened but if I tried to tell her about it, she'd never believe me. And I can't blame her.

It started while I was talking to my cellmate, Danny. I must have dozed off because I had the most lifelike dream I've ever had. I was sure we were actually there but Danny reminded me that we're both in a locked cell, so how could we be anywhere else? Let alone hundreds of years ago! I suppose he's right, but—

We were back in the time of Henry VIII and it was horrible. Everything smelled so bad, I had to keep throwing up and there was no fresh air anywhere. All the streets were covered with mud and other stuff and that's where most of the smell was coming from. But the dung cart didn't help that either.

I had to follow Danny up to this place, like a square or something and it was full of happy people. It was so sick! They were all excited like it was a fair or a celebration but it wasn't! It was the day the ex-Queen was executed by having her head chopped off; all for having an affair! I can't stop thinking about it but

Danny said if I write it down, I might be able to get it out of my mind and get some sleep.

Next thing, I'm back in the cell and I'm feeling angry that she had to die for such a stupid, little thing.

Danny says that he was just teaching me about justice! Because I'd been going on to him about how the Olds punish me and treat me like I'm a kid! Looks like I'd better be careful what I say to him from now on!

If that was their idea of justice back then, I think the curfew's not so bad after all. And I just realised maybe getting a curfew could be their way of saying that they just want to make sure I'm safe. Maybe.

But why did they leave me in jail? It feels a bit over the top to me! But s'pose I can't blame Dad or the magistrate, after all I did do it. I did break in next door and steal their car.

And yet I'm still surprised to find myself here? What did I expect?

Well, that's it for my first day, Goodnight, Diary!

*

'That's it for me tonight,' Jake says as he closes his diary and places it on his bedside table. 'I hope you're right about it taking my mind off everything. I could do with a damn good sleep.'

'You'll be right, mate. Just get some sleep and you'll remember it all as a dream in the morning.' But Jake thinks, didn't Danny just say that that's exactly what it *was,* only a dream? So, why is he saying that I'll only remember it as a dream now?

'Come on, it'll be "lights out" in a minute,' Danny says, 'I always put my book down before then because it's pitch dark in here; you can't see your hand in front of your face or I can't anyway with my dodgy eyesight.' He motions to his thick-lens glasses. 'Good night, Jake!'

'Good night, Danny, See you in the morning.'

And then Jake falls into a deep and dreamless sleep.

Chapter Six
Tuesday-Mountview

When Jake comes back into his cell early the next morning, fresh from his shower and still rubbing his wet hair vigorously with his towel, Danny is nowhere to be seen. Thinking that he must have already gone down to breakfast, he stashes his toiletries away and hastily makes his bed.

He can just hear his mother singing "This is His Once-a-Year Day!" loud and clear and he can't help but smile. She'd be proud of me today anyway, he thinks and then decides to tell her about this magnificent feat the next time he talks to her.

But then looking at his meagre attempt against Danny's perfectly made bed, he thinks he might just need a few lessons from the master before he goes around bragging about his bed-making prowess too much. Danny's blanket is so taut you could bounce a coin off it!

He walks down to breakfast wondering just when his mother actually does make his bed anyway; it's always made when he comes home from school and all his clothes have been picked up off the floor, washed, ironed and put away.

He feels ashamed that not only has he never thanked her for doing all that but most of the time, he doesn't even notice that she's done it. Spoiled brat! He just hopes it's not too late to thank her the next time he sees her instead of bragging about how *he* made his *own* bed *once*!

Arriving in the dining room, he looks around the tables to see if he can find Danny sitting at any of them but no luck. He probably finished and gone. That's OK, he'll find him later. He gets his food and sits down to eat at an almost empty table with only one old guy sitting up the other end.

He's obviously finished eating and now he's leaning back in his chair his with his steaming mug of coffee in hand, unashamedly summing Jake up from head to toe. He gulps his breakfast down nervously, hardly even stopping to chew but feeling the need to escape those piercing, rheumy old eyes as quickly as he can.

As he cleans his plate away, he thinks he may as well go out to the exercise yard and get some fresh air, maybe Danny will be out there to hang around with. He feels strangely vulnerably without Danny by his side, even a bit threatened by the once over that weather-beaten, crusty old geezer was giving him.

The glaring light is blinding when he steps into the clear morning sunshine. He tries to stay out of everyone's line of sight while he makes his way shyly around, looking for Danny and he's conscious of keeping his head down; the last thing he needs is any sort of confrontation as he knows only too well, he's out of his depth in the "who's the toughest?" stakes in here!

After he's given the yard a quick scout around with still no sign of his cellmate, he wanders back inside to the also Dannyless TV room and sits staring blankly at the screen. Currently featuring is a jovial guy talking earnestly about Funeral Plans and he thinks this advertorial seems to take on a newer, darker meaning when viewed from this vantage point.

So, he's glad for the distraction when a guard walks in and reads some names out loud to the room in general. Glad, that is, until *his* name is called and he stands nervously wondering what he's done now and how much more trouble he's in because of it!

'Aren't you lot the lucky ones? You've all got visitors. Follow me and stay in single file,' he barks. Single file? God, he hasn't heard that since primary school and he thinks his *parents* treat him like a child! What's next? Playtime?

But at least he's got a visitor, thank heavens! He hopes it's not a solicitor or something, he really needs a friendly face right now not another suit! They follow Big Chief Laugh-a-lot into a room with scattered tables and chairs and right there at the far back of the room, is his Mum.

His heart aches when he sees her sitting there all alone and looking totally out of place. He knows how hard it would have been for her to come in here this way. He walks as quickly as he can—"no running", over to her and sits at the other side of the table as directed.

He immediately tears up and is craving a reassuring hug but no contact is permitted either, so they'll just have to make the best of what they've got. He looks in cringing shame at the anguish in his mother's tear-stained face and for a moment, he can't even find his voice, let alone use it.

'How are you, Jacob? Are they treating you alright?' she manages to ask between sobs and stammers.

'Yeah, of course they are, Mum. I'm not in the full prison yet; this is just where they hold you until your case and sentencing comes up. Don't worry. I'll be OK!'

'Your father would have been here too, you know,' she continues not meeting his eyes and he thinks, 'Yeah, sure he would!', 'but he has an operation scheduled today. You know how busy he gets, oh dear,' she dissolves into tears again and wrings her hands miserably, ending up by putting them on her lap under the table so they'd be out of his sight.'

'It's OK, Mum! I'm really happy to see *you*!'

'Chelsea wanted to come too but they said no; something about this Covid business but everyone's blaming everything on *that* at the moment. And you know me, I don't know what to think.' He looks around the room and notices a conspicuous lack of anybody under eighteen. And each table does only have one visitor. Suppose they all just have to go with the flow. And one visitor's better than none at all!

'Better to be sure than sorry, eh?'

She sighs with relief and Jake realises she was actually afraid that he might cause some sort of scene or something.

'Are they feeding you, darling? You don't just get gruel and slops, do you?'

She looks so concerned and worried that he can't help laughing out loud for the first time since he's been in here. 'No, Mum! That's only on the telly. The food's pretty good actually.' She seems to be a bit miffed at that, so he jumps in, 'The helpings are nowhere near the size of yours, though but it's enough,' and he smiles at her lovingly, not saying what comes to mind next, 'nowhere near the size but a lot more edible!'

They come to a bit of a pause there for a minute, each not quite knowing what to say next, so Jake jumps in. 'Have you heard anything about Kenny? Is he OK?' he feels the tears start building again, 'Did he make it?' It'd been so hard not even knowing if he was alive or dead!

'He's still in a bad way, darling. They've put him in an induced coma so it's just a waiting game now! Something about getting the swelling to go down.'

Jake hangs his head in shame, guessing correctly that they finally went a bit too far this time! 'Can you keep me updated, *please*?'

'Of course, I can!'

There's another awkward pause and they just look deep into each other's eyes.

'I'm in with a nice guy.'

'Are you sharing with anyone?'

The questions crash into each other in a mangle of words and they both stop in their tracks, grinning.

'Yeah, Mum, his name's Danny. Seems like a nice guy and he's really interesting to talk to!'

'Interesting in a good way, I hope! I had my fingers crossed you'd at least have your own room like you do at home!' She sounds quite indignant that they haven't given Jacob a private suite.

'Mum! It's not a hotel, you know. I'm really lucky to be in with *him* and not some of the others.'

She nods her head, agreeing. 'I suppose it's better than being locked up with a great muscly, tattooed man who might do God knows what to you, if what you hear around the traps is anything to go by!'

'What "traps", Mum? And don't say the hairdresser.' So, to quieten her nerves more than anything else, he goes on to tell her all about Danny and his interest in history. Leaving out how badly the story last night had affected him. No need for her to know about that.

'What did he do to end up in here?' she asks, thinking he can't be as angelic as Jacob's making out considering where they've met.

'I don't know, Mum. He hasn't said and I figure if he wants me to know, he'll tell me. But I suppose by looking at him, it must be some sort of computer crime or maybe fraud or something like that. He doesn't seem to be much older than me but he's pretty intelligent I'd say.'

She can't hold it back this time, 'Not too intelligent to end up in here, though.'

'There's a difference between IQ smart and street smart, Mum.'

'Mm, I suppose you're right.'

He notes the hesitancy in her voice and is just wondering how else he can alleviate those worries when a guard calls out, 'Time's up. Please say your goodbyes and visitors, please make your way to the exits.'

'Thanks for coming, Mum.' He feels the tears stinging his eyes again and tries to smile through them. He doesn't want her to see him upset.

'It's OK, love. I'll be back in a couple of days and don't worry, I'm still on your father's back to pay that bail and get you out of here.'

'Well, if anyone can change his mind, I know you can.'

'You betcha! World Champion Nagger!'

They both share a nervous laugh and Jake is led away as his mother leaves the visiting area, once again sniffling into a handkerchief.

*

He flops onto an empty couch in the common room and stares blankly again at the TV, running through every nuance of their conversation and thinking regretfully about how badly he's treated her. Not to mention how guilty he feels about how upset she'd just looked. Somebody flops down beside him, interrupting his train of thought and Jake is surprised to see it's the old guy from breakfast.

'D'ya mind if I turn this over t'the footy?' His voice is no more than a croaky whisper and Jake has to strain his ears to hear what he's saying.

So caught up in his own thoughts as he was, it takes a moment for his words to even register. 'Oh sure, go for it. I wasn't really watching it anyway.'

'Thought ya looked lonely sittin' 'ere all on ya own. I'm Ernie.' Hmm, not too scary, Jake decides but he's glad he didn't hear that voice in a dark hallway in the middle of the night.

'G'Day! I'm Jake. I was looking for my cellmate, thought he might be in here by now but I can't see him anywhere!'

'Who ya in with?'

'His name's Danny. Don't know his surname.'

'Ahh, so ya're in with Danny, are ya?' he nods understandingly. 'He'll be good for ya, Danny will!'

'What do you mean?' Sounds like he knows Danny pretty well and must like him and Jake wants to know as much about Danny as he can, so he starts asking Ernie all about him.

Ernie tells him that he too was in with Danny when he first came in and he'd really helped him. Made him see that the sentence he'd been given was pretty well the right one for what he did. It made it a lot easier to stay than it would have been, that's for sure.

But other than that, he knows very little. He's learned that in here, you just take people as they come and don't ask too many questions. Jake wonders if his throat is hurting or if it's always like that.

'What did you do?' Jake asks innocently.

But Ernie just smiles and says laconically, 'Best ya don't know that, son. Just listen to Danny and ya won't go wrong!' A comfortable silence falls between the two, Jake wondering what he could have done that was so bad he can't even talk about it and Ernie travelling back through the years in his mind's eye, remembering.

*

1991

Thirty years before their conversation, Ernie had been a road worker and had been working full time, building the M5 South Western Motorway from Campbelltown to the airport and just as it was nearing completion in 1991, he spent a lot of his spare time wondering what to do next.

Christmas was approaching, a time when Ernie felt the vicious sting of loneliness most and he was considering hitting the road to look for some sort of farm work as soon as he could in order to avoid going through another silly season on his own.

He'd made some good mates while he was working on the roads but didn't feel close enough to any of them to make him want to put down roots. They could always stay in touch but he knew they wouldn't and neither would he. There's a time to everything and this time has ended, he told himself.

The last day at work was a bittersweet one. Yes, he was free to start his travelling and looking for work but with this job ending, so did his wages. At tools down, the guys all headed for the nearest pub to celebrate and the beer flowed.

At eleven o'clock that same night, Ernie comes staggering out of the pub door mumbling his own version of "We'll Meet Again" drunkenly when he bumps into his mate Bill and a couple of other guys, standing there as if they've been waiting for him.

'G'day, Bill! Aren't ya goin' 'ome, mate?' Ernie slurs.

'Nah, mate and neither are you.' What's going on, Bill doesn't even sound like he's been drinking at all but all that beer! Ernie squints his eyes as he tries

to focus on what's happening but Jack comes from the side and lands a hard blow to Ernie's jaw.

He falls to the footpath and Bill kneels on his neck, leaving Ernie struggling to breathe, while calling loudly over his shoulder to Jack.

'Quick, grab his wallet!'

Ernie wants to stop them, he tries to say, 'No, not ma wallet!' but nothing comes out of his almost collapsed vocal cords. He'd been to the bank on his way to the pub and withdrawn almost his entire termination payment.

He keeps most of his money under his bed in a tin box where he can easily get to it, not trusting the banks to keep it safe and sound but even so what they're after still amounts to nearly all his life savings.

'Get his keys as well! Thanks for the heads up about the box under ya bed, mate!' he sneers as he stands, releasing the pressure on Ernie's throat. They take off like the cowards they are, while Ernie gasps and thankfully feels the cool night air flowing in and filling his lungs.

He lies there on the asphalt footpath, gasping and flailing about like a beached fish and doesn't even notice when a couple of the other guys come laughing out of the pub and rush straight over to him, horrified. 'Ernie! You alright, mate?' He shakes his head from side to side and points repeatedly at his throat. 'Come on, Old Mate, we're gonna get you to the hospital.'

The doctors agree that he was lucky to survive the attack but he would probably never speak again and after months of rehabilitation, it looks like they might be right. He was able to tell the police who had attacked him through scribbled notes but they said without any witnesses, there wouldn't be enough to charge him. They were sorry!

'Not as sorry as Bill's gonna be!' thinks Ernie and starts planning his revenge that very same day.

Luckily one of the other guys, Paul, has a little, self-contained flat out in his back yard, The Cabana he calls it; talk about airs and graces but it's just perfect for Ernie to live in while he finishes recuperating. He goes on the pension and pays Paul a minimal weekly rent, refusing to take "charity" as he thinks of it but unknown to him, Paul has been saving this rent to give back to him in a lump sum when he leaves.

The Cabana would have been empty anyway, except for the occasional visitor and he doesn't really need Ernie's money. He'll just have to think of a way to make Ernie believe that it's rightfully his. Ernie still wants to find a job as far away from this cursed city as he can get and starts answering Job Vacancy ads in the paper each week. He's been working hard at getting some sort of voice back but in the end has to acknowledge that what he's got now is probably the best he can hope for, a rough, dry croak but at least he can communicate.

When weeks pass and he still hasn't landed any of the jobs he's applied for, his anger starts to boil up inside him again and his thirst for revenge on Bill grows even keener. He starts to hatch a plan and decides that the best idea is to keep his eyes open and his mouth shut about it all and when the time's right, he'll know it!

So, when he asks Paul one night if he'd like to come down the local for a cleansing ale or two, he's surprised by Paul's reaction.

'What's up?'

Paul looks a bit nervous, 'Yeah, sounds good. I was going down myself as it happens. A few of the other guys are coming down too tonight but I think Bill might be there.' Awkward!

Ernie surprises him with his reply, shrugging his shoulders saying, 'That's fine. All water under the bridge now, anyway.' He tells Paul he'll meet him at the car before quickly hurrying back to the Cabana on the pretext of getting his coat and puts Point One of his long thought about plan into action.

Walking into the pub, he smiles and claps everybody on the back, glad to see them and they're glad to see him too. As he gets to Bill, he smiles up at him leaving Bill confused and on the back foot. He wasn't sure which way it would go, seeing Ernie again and hopes he doesn't want his money back; that's all gone a long time ago.

But here's Ernie looking happy and almost relieved to see him. Point Two. They wrap their arms around each other the way footballers do after they've won their game and suddenly, Bill collapses to the floor, screaming in agony. Ernie's blade had slid effortlessly out of his coat sleeve where it was concealed and sliced straight into Bill's back like a hot knife through butter.

But he wasn't content to leave it there. With the other guys trying to drag him off, Ernie showed the strength of a dozen men to pull the knife out of his back and plunge it in again for a couple more well aimed strikes home. By the time the others have succeeded in pulling him away from Bill's crumpled and bloody remains, they can all see at a glance that Bill's dead.

So, Ernie ended up getting life But due to health complications, it was deemed he was safe enough to stay in the minimum-security institution while he received treatment and had proved to be a model prisoner. He's never left there. He was not a born killer but he never once regretted what he did that night.

Yes, Bill got what he deserved and as Danny had shown him later on, so did he.

*

He looks back over at Jake. This fresh-faced kid is one of the first people to sit and talk with him. Most of the other young guys that come through here seem to treat him as the butt of their jokes but Jake seems to be listening to him with a hesitant respect.

'No', he thinks, 'he doesn't need to know what I did, he really doesn't.'

*

Jake heads straight back to his room after dinner. He feels exhausted, even though he hasn't actually done anything all day and can't stand any more of the mind-numbing TV in the common room.

Danny's sitting on his bed with his head in a book and looks up smiling when Jake comes through the door. 'Hi! How was your day?'

'It was OK. Mum came to visit me but other than that I just sort of wandered around, looking for you mostly!'

'Oh well, I keep myself to myself most of the time and I spend every day in the library, so you wouldn't have found me anyway. Your day sounds a lot better.'

'I met a guy called Ernie. He said he knows you and you helped him when he was in with you.'

A huge grin splits Danny's face. 'So, Ernie's still here then, is he? Well, good for him! He'll be a good friend to you if you just stick with him. He'll look after you!'

'He said the same about you. He said stick with you and I won't go wrong!'

Danny laughs and says, 'A mutual admiration society, don't you think?' and Jake smiles and nods in return.'

Jake sits watching Danny with his head once again buried in his book and wonders why he didn't know that Ernie was still here. He's a bit of a strange one, is Danny. And how does he fill in all day, every day, in the library? Probably just reading.

'So, you're in the library every day. What do you do in there? They wouldn't let you just sit and read all day, would they?'

Danny looks up and marks his place in his book. 'No, I help out binding the books that have been damaged, updating their files and putting them back on the shelves so we know where to get them. But after that, then yes, I can read whatever I like until it's time to come back here.'

'So what do you read?'

'Guess!'

'More history?' Jake asks incredulously. How could you read history every day and not end up getting bored?

'Yep! Just more history, it's my passion.'

Jake supposes that makes sense. That must have been why he was so good at telling him all that stuff about Henry VIII and Anne Boleyn last night, just like he'd told his Mum. He's so good at telling a story that he really brings it to life! He could have done with Danny as a history teacher at school.

Mr Rowe was so boring and made everything so dry and dusty, standing at the front of the class and droning on for hour after hour. But Danny was probably already locked up in here then, so Mr Rowe it was. He just wishes he'd told him he'd be in the library in the first place, it would have saved a lot of looking around!

'I felt like a duck out of water all day, I just wish you would have been there to tell me what's what.' Oh God, grow up! He sounds like a little kid clinging to his mother's apron strings. Danny's not his security blanket, he's got problems of his own. For God's sake, suck it up, Jake!

'Don't worry, I'll always end up here each night, no matter what. And Ernie could probably do a better job looking after you than me anyway.'

'Well, we'll both end up here every night, won't we?' Jake tries to sound more adult and accepting. But then spoils the illusion with a whingey, 'Might as well be back *home*!'

'What do you mean? I thought you were happy to see your mother today.'

'Yeah, I was. And I mean it's not Mum's fault, she can't help it. Dad's the one who calls all the shots. He says, jump! And Mum just says, "How high?"

She goes along with whatever he says. It's probably a lot easier than fighting with him. But still, it doesn't make my life any easier, does it? Sometimes I wish she'd stand up for *us* a bit more.'

'Us? Who's us?'

'Me and my sister, Chelsea.'

'And stand up for what?'

'Huh, where do I start? My room's not any bigger than this cell, to start with. *And* I have to share my bathroom with Chelsea. Can you imagine it? Mess *everywhere* and some of it's just plain embarrassing!'

'So, sharing your bathroom with your sister is *it?* That's the *extent* of your problems?'

'No, it's just, oh I don't know, it's the whole thing; you wouldn't understand! I mean, even the food we get dished up every night. Poor old Mum's not much of a cook and I know she tries but it's just the same-old-same-old every night of the bloody week. Would you believe, the food's actually better in here? I tell my mates at school it's like living in third world conditions living at my place.'

'I don't know about third world living conditions but in the library today, I was reading about how people actually lived and worked right here in Sydney back in the mid-nineteenth century and believe me, it wasn't pretty!'

'Who cares?'

Danny thinks that Jake will definitely care when he's done with him.

'OK, let me set the scene. Back then, Queen Victoria was on the throne and all the people really loved her, she was a very popular Queen. But along with Fitzroy, the Governor, they couldn't do much about the conditions the normal people were faced with. They were—'

His voice fades and Jake sits listening intently, gradually feeling himself succumb once again to the soothing lull of Danny's precise, British accent. He starts feeling so tired that he's finding it hard to keep his focus and then his eyes close.

Chapter Seven
1851-Sydney, Australia

When Jake opens his eyes, it takes them a few seconds to adjust to the bright, glaring light of a beautiful, sunny Sydney day. The water on the harbour is sparkling like it's covered in a million tiny diamonds and the sounds of the busy wharves all around him are deafening.

He looks in awe at the huge, old sailing ships swaying and rocking rhythmically in the docks while an army of hardened men scurry up and down the gangplanks, unloading cargo onto waiting horse-drawn carts. From there, it'll all be taken to either market for sale or warehouses to be stored.

Men and women who look like they're dressed in period costume are all hurrying to and fro with their manservants toting heavy, fully laden trunks behind them.

'Where are we now? This looks like the harbour, so we must be in Sydney but where *exactly* are we?' he turns to ask Danny. At that same moment, he spies hordes of filthy rats running around between their feet and narrowly missing the passing hooves of the carriage horses. Gross!

'You're right, we are in Sydney, Circular Quay actually but right now, it's still known as Semi Circular Quay. Looks a bit different, eh?'

'I thought we must have been further around. It's all so *dirty*! This doesn't look like Circular Quay at all. And what do you mean, "right now"?'

'It's 1851, Jake. The Quay's a lot different to what you know now.' He looks at the surprise on Jake's face and doesn't need to wait for a reply to that revelation.

Jake turns his nose up as he takes in the state of the street, dirty and grimy but miles better than London was last time. Although there is still the pervasive aroma of unwashed labourers and rotting cabbage! Why is it always cabbage? he wonders.

'Did everywhere smell this bad back in the old days?'

'Probably.'

He hadn't realised he'd said that out loud but he starts looking at it again through his twenty-first century eyes. He knows the Quay very well and he's trying to work out exactly where they're standing. He looks over to Benelong Point where the Opera House proudly stands today and it's empty.

He quickly swings and looks behind him, expecting to see the Harbour Bridge joining north to south but again nothing. He is, however, surprised to see that The Rocks don't seem to be much different. So, something has survived, at least.

Danny watches him closely. He sees him looking this way and that and can see the confusion at every turn when he realises that nothing is as it should be. He knows just what he's thinking and sees him taking in the "before" with his eyes and the "after" with his mind, comparing the two and finding the former sadly lacking.

A wave of homesickness washes over Jake and as he lifts his arm to his face, he stops short, looking in wonder at the cream full-sleeved shirt he's wearing. His eyes immediately travel down to take in the rest of his outfit, tatty old trousers are beneath the calico shirt and an apron of all things is tied around his waist!

'Why am I dressed like this?' he asks Danny, who's still sporting his prison greens!

'And you're *not*?'

Danny explains that Jake actually has a job working in a grand house in Macquarie St, it's owned by the very strict factory owner, Ambrose Ross; so they'd better get a wriggle on and get him back to work before anybody notices he's missing. Jake is alarmed at this turn of events.

'Aren't you coming with me?' he can't expect him to do this on his *own*! What's his job? Where does he live when he's not working? How long will Danny be away? And if Danny's not coming to take him back, then how's he going to get back on his own?

'Hey, one thing at a time. First of all, No, I will not be coming with you but that's not to say I won't be keeping an eye on you. Some things you just have to see and understand for yourself. You'll be fine, don't worry. In these days, someone like you, who does a general dogsbody type of job, would live where you work. And you don't have to worry about going back on your own. I promise, you'll be all right.'

They arrive at a spacious, white dwelling which seems to Jake to be right across from where the Conservatorium of Music is today and Jake goes to walk straight up the front stairs. 'Not that way, young Jake!' Danny grabs hold of him and pulls him to the side.

'*You're* round the *back*.'

He walks him around to the servants' entrance with a 'Look after yourself, I'll be back,' and Jake stands forlornly watching him walk off down the path to Macquarie St until he turns and disappears from view behind the building. He looks at a rather large and imposing door with a loud ruckus in process behind it and pushes it open with trepidation.

He walks in and stands staring, he's in a massive kitchen, full to overflowing with cooks and maids bustling over steaming pots and boiling kettles in the fireplace. He has no idea what he's supposed to do next, so he stays standing where he is looking and feeling incredibly stupid!

It looks like everybody else has a purpose and knows exactly what they should be doing except him! A young maid comes over to him and grabs him by the arm.

'Jacob, th'old man's been yellin' for ya all aft'noon. Ya're in for it, mate! Might be best if ya made yaself scarce.'

'Lilian!' shouts what looks like the head cook, 'Get away from 'im, NOW. He's got hisself in this trouble, you just look after *your*self so ya don't end up in the same boat.'

'Yes, Cook,' she answers, giving him an urgent flick of her head towards the back door, she drops her head and quickly returns to her station at the chopping board.

Jake wonders what sort of trouble he's in now. Not again! And he's trying to decide whether to take Lilian's advice or not; surely that would only make the old guy angrier, when a tall, straight man enters the room hollering, 'Jacob!'

Everybody jumps and then quickly averts their eyes, desperate not to bring any attention to themselves and every person to a tee applies themselves to their jobs with renewed vigour.

Ambrose Ross is an imposing figure of a man, Jake thinks he must be over six feet tall and dressed in black, with a walking stick which he seems to wield like a weapon, all complemented by a ferocious scowl on his weathered old face.

'Too late,' he says to himself.

'*Where have you been*? I've been calling for you for the last hour and now I've had to come to look for you *myself*! And you know what that means!'

Jake didn't but had a pretty good idea that he was about to find out. The infuriated Master kicks open a narrow door in the side wall which reveals a rickety staircase leading down to what Jake can only guess is the basement. He pulls Jake over to it by the scruff of his neck and just about pushes him down the stairs, beating him at every step with his stick.

When Jake lands at the bottom of the stairs in a heap on the floor, the beating continues, the stick alternating with vicious kicks to his ribs and back, until Jake thinks he can't stand it any longer and that old Ross is going to keep going until he's broken every bone in Jake's body.

But through years of experience, the cagey old bully knows better than that. Inflict the most pain without any real damage is his motto. If he goes too far, he won't be getting any work out of this snivelling creature until he heals, so as always, he knows just when to stop.

'Get upstairs and light the fire in the library *NOW!* And never cause me to lose my temper like that again. *Do you understand*?'

'Yes, sir!'

'*LOUDER!*'

'YES, SIR!' Jake calls out like an obedient soldier and starts crawling away, expecting the cane to come down on his back again at any moment.

'*Now*, you've got until the count of ten to get back to work or there'll be more where that came from. ONE!'

Jake scampers back up the stairs, wincing in pain all the way and still terrified about what to expect from the crazy old thug who's following closely behind.

'TWO!'

And Jake's up the next flight of stairs in an instant, wasting no time looking for the library. He fiddles a bit getting the fire lit, he's never had to light a fire in his life but with that job finally accomplished, he's dispatched back downstairs again; this time to chop more wood to keep the household warm and fed.

As he starts his descent back into the basement with the last armload of firewood for the stockpile, he desperately hopes this is his last chore for the day. He's aching all over. Where's Danny? He's really had enough of this and he's yearning to return to the comfort and security of their shared cell. But to his dismay, standing at the bottom of the stairs is the master grinning at him and showing all his rotten teeth in their full, repulsive glory.

'No comfy bed for you tonight, maybe now you'll learn your lesson and a bit of respect as well!'

He grabs Jake and forcefully throws him back against the wall, knocking the breath out of him and clasping something around each wrist as he does. He's so strong and he takes Jake so much by surprise that he realises he didn't even try to offer any resistance but when he tries to move away from the wall, he finds he's chained to it by his clamped wrists and Ross is walking up the stairs.

He calls out, 'Sweet dreams!' in a garishly loving voice as he goes, before slamming the door shut and leaving Jake in total and blinding darkness, listening to the scurrying feet of a horde of rats.

*

Ambrose Ross runs a factory supplying bricks and tiles to the growing construction companies. Sydney's population is growing so quickly that there's a great demand for housing. To keep his own costs down, he employs a great number of children, some as young as four years old and he works them mercilessly to the bone for up to fourteen hours a day and all for a couple of lousy pennies.

Of course, as soon as they reach adult level wages, he just replaces them with new children from the street. He constantly brags about the fact that he works his employees, both at the factory and at home, until they drop and doesn't see anything wrong with that. Their conditions are nothing if not bleak. But he won't let anyone say he starves them, his pride just won't allow that!

So early the next morning, Lilian gingerly opens the door to the basement and starts carefully picking her way down the stairs. These rotten old steps are not stable at the best of times! But this morning, she's carrying some precious cargo, as well as some that's definitely not-so-precious.

She carefully balances a mug of water, holding it with both hands and trying not to spill even a single precious drop, which she thinks he must be needing badly by now. 'The master said this is ta be ya breakfast today, Jacob!' she looks at him, sorrow etched in every line of her face and pulls a chunk of mouldy maggot-ridden stale bread from her apron pocket.

His eyes grow wide in horror and he opens his mouth to protest but she shushes him and smiling, she takes out two large freshly baked biscuits and smuggles them over to him, saying Cook couldn't stand by and see him eat that filth.

'But don't leave no crumbs or he'll beat ya again *and* me *and* Cook most like! And better be quick with 'em, 'e'll be down soon 'nough, I 'spect to take off ya chains so ya can get back ta work.' Message and breakfast both delivered safely, she scurries back up the stairs and out into the already bustling kitchen.

He makes short work of gobbling the biscuits down and gulping all the water too just in case the "Master" thinks he shouldn't have that either. No way is that evil old man going to take anything from him this morning.

And before Lillian and Cook can be in trouble as well, he hides the stale bread deep down in his large pants pocket, hoping against hope that he doesn't leave a trail of crumbs from the small hole in his pocket as he walks!

*

His first job of the day is to go to the butcher's shop in King St and bring back a half carcass of beef for Cook. She's bent on preparing a roast for the family's dinner that night and also to work her magic stretching the rest of it out over the next week.

Jake thanks heaven he's out of that house of horrors and silently sends up more thanks for the sweet Lillian. Where would he have been without her? He relieves himself of the maggoty bread where he's sure Ambrose Bloody Ross will never find it and continues on his way quickly!

With that mission accomplished, he comes out of the butcher shop and starts back to the house as fast as his feet will take him on the slippery, muddy roads with the beef hanging around his shoulders.

He knows he can't be late, for fear of another flogging and he's so intent on the job at hand that he doesn't even see the horse drawn carriage come careening wildly around the corner and only vaguely hears someone shout, 'Watch out, boy!'

In his confusion and haste he turns quickly, dropping the meat and stands stock still in the middle of the road, staring at the muddied mess at his feet and shaking uncontrollably just knowing what this will mean.

The horse is also confused by Jake's sudden stop right in front of him and while trying to slow itself down to bring the carriage to a halt, it rears onto its hind legs just a few inches away from the frozen, stunned boy.

The horse's forelegs are clawing at the air, trying to find purchase but finding none, they start to descend with a terrifying force right onto Jake's waiting torso! He raises his arms in a useless effort to shield himself from the inevitable blow when suddenly, he feels himself being pulled roughly out of the way.

And he blacks out.

When he comes to, he and Danny are back in their cell and he's safe, sound and clean. Danny still has a firm grip on his raised right arm and Jake's still trembling and shaking his head to try to clear that terrifying vision.

Slowly, the world blacks out again and a peaceful silence closes in.

Chapter Eight
2022-Mountview

Jake slowly opens his eyes and struggles to take in what he's seeing. It looks like a disembodied *head* and it's hovering directly in front of his face. He can't quite focus on it, so he closes his eyes frowning and hopes it'll be gone when he dares to look again.

But when he does sneak another peek, it's *still there;* although this time, thankfully, it's firmly attached to the body of a very concerned Danny. His mouth is moving but Jake can't make out what he's trying to tell him. What's he saying? he thinks, as he struggles to hear the words but it's all just garbled nonsense and it sounds like it's coming from somewhere far away and through a very long and foggy tunnel.

'Jake! Jake! Come on mate, wake up!' Danny taps his cheek lightly, trying to bring him out of it and Jake gradually responds, coming round and looking up at him questioningly and still very shaken.

'Wha' happened?' he asks foggily and looking to his side, he sees that he's lying on the floor. What's he doing down here? He tries to sit up but a stabbing pain shoots through his neck and into his head, stopping him in his tracks. He slumps back down helplessly surrendering to it.

'You fainted, mate! Again! You really should have that looked at! And by the size of that lump on your forehead, you must have clocked it pretty hard when you fell!'

He struggles to a sitting position leaning against the bed. Danny thinks it's probably best to leave him as he is for a while but when he sees the colour coming back into his cheeks, he helps him up and onto the bed.

'Jake, look at me! Do you have any double vision or anything?'

'No, no, I'm fine!' he snaps pulling away from him as Danny tries to look for signs of a concussion or any other injury. But he looks okay and his speech is pretty clear and not slurred, so he goes back over to his own bed as Jake mumbles, 'Sorry, it's just a headache! I'll be right.'

Danny picks up his library book, pushes his glasses back up his nose and starts reading while Jake sits stock still, trying to remember what he was doing before he fainted.

What caused it? And *then* he remembers!

'What the *hell* were you *thinking*?' he erupts. '*Leaving* me there in that *bloody house* on my *own*?' He sounds like a petulant child but he doesn't care. 'I could have been *killed*!'

'No, you *couldn't*, Jake. We never left this cell. I was here with you the whole time.'

That's it! Jake's had enough! 'Stop *saying* that, will you? You know as well as I do, where we were. You left me on that bloody doorstep and took off, just left me there to get beaten and starved and chained to a wall in that bloody basement all night!'

Infuriatingly, Danny just smiles back at him. He thinks I'm exaggerating, Jake fumes. Somehow not being believed is worse than what had actually happened and Danny's reaction only serves to make him even *more* furious.

'Here, look at these bruises if you don't believe me.' He lifts his sweatshirt to reveal a clear, unblemished midriff, his skin as smooth and soft as a new-born baby. The only bruises he can find anywhere on his body are the remnants of his altercation with the parked car.

Danny watches the strange twisting, turning dance Jake's performing in search of an evidential bruise or two and raises his eyebrows.

'What the—? Look, I don't know what's going on here,' Jake cries out, 'but I'm not doing it anymore! I want *out,* this is all just getting too *weird*. I'm *out*! How do I get a transfer to another cell?' He starts banging on the cell door shouting, 'Guard, Guard!' at the top of his voice.

'Settle down, mate. We *all* want out and you can't just "get a transfer". Look at you, there's nothing wrong with you, you're probably safer here than out on the streets or even, don't forget, in another cell. Just sit down and relax and tell me what happened, what you think you "saw" and start at the beginning.'

Jake settles down a bit but still looks sullen and wary as he describes everything that happened to him in full detail from the moment Danny left him for dead outside on the doorstep to the rearing horse about to trample him into the dirt!

'And then I woke up *here*, on the *floor* with *your* face floating in the air in front of my very eyes. What the hell happened? And don't say it was a dream, it *wasn't* a dream. If it wasn't for Lillian and Cook, I'd probably be dead.'

Danny just shakes his head, he can't convince him that he hasn't left the cell but if he's living all of this in his own mind and learning from it, then so be it. He tries a different tack.

'You know, that is exactly how they all *did* live back then. The masters had all the power and the workers were just there to work their fingers to the bone, no thanks, just lucky to have a job at all. They were thought of as no more than tools or machines to make the *master's* lives more comfortable.

'They had absolutely no rights whatsoever and when they dropped to the ground in sheer exhaustion, they were just kicked to the kerb and a new guy'd be picked out of the gutter to do the job. Can you believe most of them were actually *thankful* for their food and board and the pittance of a wage they were given at the end of each week?'

'Food and board? That's a laugh! My "board" was a cold stone wall in a pitch-black basement full of rats! And the only "food" he gave me was rotting, maggot-infested bread. Thank god for Cook's biscuits.'

'Hmm, well, at least you had that. And you know what? The bedroom you would have been given wouldn't've been much better. It wouldn't have been any warmer or lighter than where you ended up and not much bigger than a cupboard either.'

Jake sits solemnly staring at the floor, lost in thought. 'Unbelievable! How could people live like that?'

'Lots of times, they didn't. They couldn't! But, you're right; by these day's standards, it is unbelievable. And it'd be hard for you to compare the real difference in the workplaces since you haven't actually had a job yet.'

'Well, I wasn't going to do just anything, was I?' He looks over at Danny, 'What about you? What did you do? You probably just had it cushy with your father owning the farm and everything.'

'Nope, not at all. I was luckier than most kids in one way, though. Whitegum Station was my first job and it was a bloody long way away from home but it turned out to be the best possible place I could have asked for to start my working life!'

Danny

'*Muck out the stables, will ya Danny, then you can help us get these sheep in,*' *Mr Robertson calls out to him in a stern voice; nothing like the normally polite and gentle tone he knows from the dinner table or the library.*

'*Right sir.*' *That had taken him by surprise. He felt a bit miffed that that was the job he'd been given to do this morning. Muck out the stables? But then he thought determinedly, 'Well, you have to start somewhere! Just get stuck in and show them what you can do.' He knows he'll have to learn all aspects of running a farm "down under" and he supposes this is the best way to do it.*

The days pass by in a blur of hard physical labour in the hot sun, only made easier by the companionable banter of the other workmen and the excellent food coming out from the kitchen three times a day. Mr Robertson proves to be a hard boss but a fair one and the guys all try to do their best for him. It is almost as if his approval means just as much to them as their pay packets at the end of each week.

Danny's enjoying the workout the job is giving him too and as a result, he's quickly filling out, growing muscles on his muscles, as he'd told his Father in his last letter but he needs more than that. He's always been a top student academically and he feels his mind stagnating through lack of use and knows that his brain needs just as much stimulation as his biceps!

The library off the dining room proves to be a godsend; full of both fiction and non-fiction and the books are all laid out in clear categories. He has full run of it and Janet is enormously pleased to see him browsing, selecting and then spending happy hours reading during his time off.

Cheryl is always to be found curled up at his feet like a cat, with her head stuck in one of the many fiction novels adorning the lower shelves, both of them sipping hot drinks and sporadically remarking on something that has caught their attention.

After his nightly conversations with Mr Robertson about the history of the station had piqued his interest, he'd gone straight to the history section and had decided that the time was perfect to delve into the history of Australia as a nation, a subject they only touched on at school when discussing the British acquisition of the various colonies.

He becomes absorbed in this new interest, frequently and excitedly discussing various events and important steps in the development of this young country with his boss on the veranda each night, while contentedly sipping an after-dinner port or cognac.

'I'm terribly ignorant on the subject, I'm ashamed to say,' Cheryl confessed one night when they were knee deep in the Eureka Stockade. 'I always thought it was so dull and boring but you make it really interesting, Danny. I wish I could learn more but it's too late now!'

'It's never too late, Cher,' he enthuses, using the family's pet name for her, 'I could have a go at teaching you, if you want?'

'Would you? That would be fabulous! When can we start, tomorrow afternoon?'

Her parents both laugh, telling her to hold her horses a bit and don't crowd "Poor Danny" although Danny wouldn't have minded being crowded by Cheryl one little bit and they turn to Danny asking where he's been right through her schooling? They sure could have used him! For some strange reason that Danny couldn't fathom, Cheryl had blushed at that and hurried off into her bedroom.

And so began Danny's teaching career. Cheryl proved to be a bright girl who quickly not only absorbed but also understood, everything Danny was teaching her.

'You've got a knack for this, Cher. Too many history students think that it's enough just to memorise a page of dates and they think that's their history learned; done and dusted. But you've got a way of putting it all into perspective and understanding how it all came about. It's a real pleasure helping you.'

She had blushed again at this and Danny felt his heart melt just a little, she looked so cute when she blushed!

Mr Robertson had been observing the interaction between the teacher and the pupil and realised he was wasting Danny's talents mucking out stables and fixing fences and as he and Janet had been actively looking to hire a tutor for the twins, maybe young Daniel might be just the ticket. After all, who better to teach them than someone the kids already know and will listen to?

Danny jumps at the chance to swap farm work for teaching. Not just because it was indoors and away from the searing sun and those annoying little bush flies that crawl into your eyes and nose but also because it was something he felt truly passionate about and the thought of being able to share this with young, enquiring minds was really very exciting to say the least.

The boys thrive under Danny's tutelage and sometimes Cheryl sits in too, which Danny has to admit he finds a bit distracting but nevertheless, they all enjoy their classes and their grades slowly improve.

The boys regularly tune into "The School of the Air" for their lessons as well, as this is just about the only way children in remote areas can receive their schooling. Their teacher from "The School" was extremely pleased with their results, even congratulating Danny on how well he'd done with them.

Danny and Cheryl grow closer and closer through their classes and discussions and start spending more and more time together with their feelings for each other blossoming.

From their first romantic picnic dinner under the stars, to numerous parties and balls on neighbouring properties, they were never far apart and the single girls from miles around were seething with jealousy that Cheryl had nabbed herself such a gorgeous and devoted beau.

Cheryl did notice the frowns and turned backs of her normally happy and welcoming friends but Danny was completely unaware of the constant undercurrents and quickly made friends with the other young guys while enjoying himself enormously.

One night as the two lovebirds are sitting shoulder to shoulder on the top veranda step stargazing, Cheryl turns to him and without preamble demands, 'Are you ever going to ask me to marry you? Or do I have to bite the bullet and ask you myself?'

Danny's taken aback again at how straightforward she's being but reminds himself, for the hundredth time that things work very differently down here! He laughs in surprise and accepts without delay before she changes her mind and they immediately run in laughing, hand in hand, to tell the Robertson's their good news.

He lies awake night after night, thinking and worrying about what this new turn of events will mean to his life and how different his life will be compared to how he thought it would play out when he'd first arrived here. When he came to Australia, he was sure that it would only be for the twelve months of the agreement.

And then, with the end of that first year closing in on him, he'd decided to stay on for a while before heading home to take the reins of the family estate. But becoming engaged to Cheryl would definitely change all that now. Life surely does look rosy!

'I did go for a job in Woolies a while ago,' Jake continues, breaking into his reverie and bringing him back to reality with a thud. 'But they wanted me to start by stacking shelves. No way was I going to do that *and* work on weekends! Ha! Weekends are *mine!*'

'It's called starting at the bottom, mate and working your way up. If you weren't prepared to do those jobs, how could you ever lead a team to do them later on? You have to know what's going on every step of the way,' Danny reasons but Jake's just shaking his head.

'But I didn't want to work at Woolies for the rest of my life anyway, so what was the point?' He looks to Danny for some support that he's doing the right thing.

'The point is that the skills you were learning there would have stayed with you forever. No matter where you end up or what you end up doing, the same principals always apply. I came out to learn as much as I could at Whitegum and although farming is very different back home, I knew I could always adapt the skills I learned to what I'd be doing with our place.

'And I always thought that when I got back home, that's what I'd be doing. Just as my dad did before me. Do you see what I'm saying?' No answer, so he looks over at the stubborn young face and can just about read his mind. He's determined not to take anything positive from his work experience at Woolworths and there's nothing he can do about it.

He realises that no amount of talking is going to make Jake see any differently, so he pulls out his latest book and opens it, as if to signify the end of that conversation.

After a few more minutes thought, Jake pulls his diary out too. 'I've got to write all this down. Get my head around it!'

*

Dear Diary

Day Two, Tuesday.

Another crazy day in paradise!

Today, I went back to Sydney in 1851. Danny said I didn't but I know I did. Talk about strange! I was working for this cruel old nut job who beat me up and chained me to a wall in his basement and left me there all night with the rats!

And then, in the morning a young girl called Lillian smuggled down a couple of biscuits for me from Cook because "The Master" had told them to give me stale bread crawling with live maggots! I would have gone hungry rather than eat that! Those two saved my life but they'll never know it.

And I'd been whingeing to Danny again about Mum's cooking! Can you believe it? When I think about what people used to eat in those days, I'll never complain about what I get again. At least I know one thing for sure, it'll never be crawling with maggots!

I might even learn to cook a few things myself! Come to think about it, a lot of the chefs on the telly are guys and they've got girls falling all over them! Chef Jake-the Chick Magnet! Good name for a TV show, eh?

And that's another thing, I'll never complain about the size of my bedroom again or how I've got to share a bathroom with Chelsea. God, when I think about all that now, I can't believe how lucky I am to have what I've got! This cell is about the same size as my room but there are two of us in here, so I should just shut up about that!

And there's nothing wrong in the bathroom that a bit of organisation won't fix. I've been so wrapped up in how bad I've got it that I haven't been able to see the real problem! First thing when I get home, I'll measure it up and see where we could fit another set of drawers, one set each!

That might help for a start! And maybe I'll give Chelsea a few tips on picking up after herself too for a change! Ha-ha! Big joke!

The thing that really got to me most was the night in the basement. I could barely move my arms and had to stand like that all night. I'm ashamed to say I wet myself. I don't know if it was from fear or the cold. I couldn't get to the pot in the corner, so I thought I was going to get another beating for that as well. And that's when it hit me.

Freedom or lack of it! I wasn't even free to go to the toilet! All my life, I've had freedom to come and go as I please whenever I want, eat what I want, sleep in my own bed and yep, even to complain when I want and I could do it all without the fear of being beaten or worse, killed!

I didn't realise how much I took for granted and how much I really needed that freedom until now!

Good night, Diary.

*

He tucked his diary away and settled down for the night.

'Good night, Danny!' He figured there was no use saying, 'See you in the morning,' as he knew he wouldn't.

'Night, Jake.'

Chapter Nine
Wednesday-Mountview

Jake opens his eyes and stares at the bare cream wall of his cell. He wishes he was looking out his bedroom window, another thing he's taken for granted. He stretches and realises that he's feeling great! Wide awake, full of beans and ready to take on the day.

As he rolls over, he sees that Danny's bed is already made and momentarily wonders how he manages to get out of the cell so early every morning without waking him; must just be years of practice.

He still has time before he has to jump out of bed, so he lies back down and looks up at the ceiling, thinking. His mind drifts back over his latest adventure, only now it's taken on the fractured quality of a partially remembered dream. Did it really happen? He knows that last night he was adamant that it had!

But if it did, then *how* did it? And why does he feel so good this morning? He should be an exhausted wreck! Well, he thinks, whether it happened or not, it's only ended up making him feel even more homesick. He misses his own home, his own room and his Mum, Chelsea of all people and even his dad.

He knows he drives his father mad most of the time but he also now knows for sure he can always count on his dad to look after him, even when he's in trouble! He shudders again as memories of the horrendous conditions he'd endured push back to the front of his mind; that much he does remember and he vows to feel nothing but never-ending gratitude for everything in his life from now on.

Up and heading off to the shower, his bed made and a spring in his step, he decides to find the library and ask Danny what he's reading today. He thinks he might try to read up on the same subject every day, so they can be on the same page each night, literally.

He keeps his eyes peeled for any sign of it on his way down from the shower to breakfast but no luck. 'Ernie, where's the library?' he asks through a mouthful of something that might be either scrambled eggs or a naïve attempt at an omelette.

'Ya can't go to t'library, mate. It's not a real library anyway, not like you're thinkin', more like a storage room. Ya want somethin' ta read, there's books on those bookshelves at the back o'the TV room. Just pick anything ya want from there. They swap 'em over every Monday,' he answers as he attacks a rubbery strip of bacon.

'Ta!' Jake gets out between mouthfuls. Breakfast is not so good today, must be someone different doing the cooking but then in his mind's eye, he sees very clearly the squirming maggots in the pale grey chunk of bread and renews his attack of the remainder of his now seemingly luxurious meal with gusto!

His stomach full, he slopes into the TV room and flops on the lounge. He's confused and his mind's whirling with unanswered questions. If they can't *ever* go to the library, then just where *is* Danny? And where's he really been going that's such a big secret? Has he been lying to him? But why would he? What's the point?

Well, he's not wasting any more time looking for him today, he'll just have to ask him about it tonight. He wanders over to the bookshelves and finds a murder mystery to keep him entertained even though, he thinks, this probably isn't the best place to read it!

*

'What are you reading?' Danny looks over at him, impressed that Jake's reading anything at all; he didn't have him pegged as a bookworm!

'Murder in the High Country,' Jake answers. 'Best I could find in the bookcase; evidently *we* can't go to the library, so we just have to make do with what's on the shelf,' he adds pointedly. 'Danny, if none of us are allowed to go there, how come *you've* been getting in? What makes you so special that you can go in and we can't?'

'It's my job, mate. Don't worry, I'm no more special than anybody else in here. Everybody has to work at some stage. Suppose you'll be given something to do in the next couple of days too! I'm just happy I got the library, I love it!'

'Yeah, right up your alley. Do you get paid for working there all day, every day?'

'Yeah, a bit, not that I need it. I don't smoke or anything, so I don't need any for that. No, I just do it because I love being around books. And I get to spend my lunchtime reading whatever I want, too. *Every* day. Heaven!'

'Working for the love of it? Sorry but *that does not compute*!' He says in a mock robotic voice, 'Not in this little brain anyway!'

Danny looks over to him, 'Haven't you got an "after school" job back home?' He can't help but think that Jake couldn't be enjoying it much if he does.

'Oh God, no! The "Olds" have been pestering at me to get one for the last couple of years. But I reckon, why should I? I've got to study you know, so I don't have any spare time for that sort of rubbish!'

Danny doubts Jake would be burning the midnight oil studying either, he just doesn't seem to be a studious kind of kid. 'What do you do for spending money or don't you have any spare time for socialising either?'

'Haha! Very funny! Mum and Dad give me money whenever I want it and *of course,* I socialise! All work and no play makes Jake a dull boy! Nah, Dad's filthy rich, rollin' in it. So, he doesn't miss it. And besides, they're the ones who wanted kids! You can't have kids and see them go without life's basics, can you?' He laughs, thinking how clever that was.

Danny is gobsmacked! It's clear that Jake has always been very spoiled and because of that, he has little or no work ethic and no real idea of working to actually earn whatever he wanted or needed in his life. Just put your hand out and you're given it, right? He frowns and tries to frame his answer but where does he begin?

'Well, thing is mate, that's OK for now but you never know when your very survival may depend on earning enough money to keep yourself fed and clothed, let alone anything else! What do you spend your money on now?'

Jake shrugs, 'Takeaways, drinks, apps and any that's left over, I put through the pokies down the local pub. Now that I'm over 18, I can!'

'Yes, you can but it's not actually compulsory.' Let that sink in! 'Do you ever win?'

'Nah, never!' Jake laughs.

'And you never will! Gambling's a mugs game, young Jake!' Danny shakes his head hoping he'll learn before it gets too much of a hold on him. 'What about your clothes, shoes, school costs, things like that?'

Jake barks a derisive guffaw and says, 'Mum and Dad pay for all that stuff! *My* money is *fun* money!'

'Oh, I see!' Danny looks pensive.

'What?' Jake asks. 'What's that look for?'

'Well, it's just that everything you've been saying just reminds me of something I was reading about today. You've had such a life of luxury compared to other kids and you don't even know it!'

Jake feels a bit miffed at this. Danny's making him feel like a naughty kid or a criminal again just for taking what his parents willingly give him! He's no different to all his school friends, they don't work either and get their "pocket money" each week too just like he does, so he doesn't know who Danny's talking about but what's it got to do with him anyway?

'What other kids? I don't even know what you're talking about.'

'Well, I started off by reading about the 1929 Wall St Stock Market Crash. And then that led to the effects and consequences on millions of people, rich *and* poor. Thousands of "investors"-a fancy name for gamblers, by the way were left bankrupt and destitute, even leading to some of them committing suicide! So, the life you're describing just reminds me of those people before the crash but after the crash? You couldn't be further away from it if you tried.'

Again, Jake feels a knot of guilt tie up his insides. But then NO, why should he feel guilty this time? Surely that was all their own fault and what does Danny think he's going to do about it now anyway?

Danny starts by outlining the history of the crash that started it all and Jake relaxes, falling under his spell once again. He's gradually aware of sleep closing in, his eyes becoming heavy, his breathing becoming shallow and Danny's words becoming even more jumbled and he tries hard to concentrate on what he's saying until his eyes finally close altogether and his mind drifts.

Chapter Ten
1929-New York

Jake looks around the unfamiliar room, totally bewildered and once again no sign of Danny. Wherever he is and whatever's going to happen to him this time, he's on his own again and he'll just have to make his own way through it!

Looking around, he sees he's in a cruddy little room, gloomy as well thanks to the dim light emanating from the solitary, uncovered light globe hanging from the ceiling. He's sitting on a single bed with a lumpy kapok mattress covered by an old-fashioned candlewick bedspread, so thin you could see light through it and a stained and barely-there pillow sitting pathetically at one end.

'Boy, this really is cheapsville!' he thinks as he takes in the old, chipped wooden furniture and filthy dirty windows. The room smells of cabbage cooking of all things and with the window stuck tight with layers and layers of decades old paint, he decides to get outside as quickly as possible to get some fresh air.

He walks over to the door, stomping on a couple of rogue cockroaches on the way but as he reaches for the handle, he jumps back in fright as a loud pounding rattles the door in its frame and threatens to take it right off its hinges.

BANG! *BANG*! *BANG*!

'I want me rent, an' I want it *NOW*! Ya hear me?' a rough voice bellows through the thin pine door.

Rent? What rent? What's going on? Where is he? Jake tiptoes softly back to the bed as the ranting, raving and cursing continues and stays as quiet as a mouse until it all subsides.

'I know ya there! Open this bloody door *NOW*!'

But Jake's planted himself back on the bed, sitting with his hands firmly covering both ears and resolutely *not* opening the door! And he's decided he's not going to either, not until he knows what's going on. After what seems like ages, the banging stops and he hears the heavy footfall of the landlord traipsing back down the stairs.

But still, he doesn't move. He sits, frozen with fear, right through the afternoon and twilight and as a full, black night emerges, he packs his things into a single meagre suitcase and quietly creeps down the stairs and out the front door.

Stepping into the street, his eyes widen in fright at all the people running wildly around as if they're in a panic, bumping into each other with some physically pushing others out of the way. A clanging bell heralds the approach of an ambulance but that only causes more confusion as people start to break away and scatter in all directions.

Jake looks up and sees the vintage ambulance trying to weave its way through the throng. 'Not another one!' mutters a stranger walking past in the opposite direction, more to himself than to anybody else. Another what? Jake wonders, before he starts to pick up threads of conversation along the way.

'Another jumper,' he hears one woman say to her friend as they scurry past.

'Not Richard from the club?' Two men walking past in the opposite direction have just heard the news. 'Yep, lost everything!'

He puts his head down to avoid the vacant, frightened faces of the passers-by and starts to follow the long, lonely road out of town and as far away from that hell of a place as possible.

*

Hours later, he stands on top of a hill looking back over the city, feeling anxious and uncertain. What's Danny landed him in this time? He was talking about the Wall St Crash when he left him and as he's checked his pockets three times and only found a dime, a lousy ten cents, he figures he must be slap bang in the middle of *that*.

Now, looking back over the view, he concludes that it must be New York. He wishes he had his phone or even a camera, no-one would believe this. The skyline is so *low,* almost non-existent, with the Empire State Building still in the process of being built!

'No use looking back that way, kid!' Jake turns quickly and sees that the owner of the voice is what he thinks is a rough looking hobo. 'Turn your back on all that and just keep looking forward, it's the only way! Where are you headed?'

'I don't know, sir.' Jake feels like he's five years old, lost, confused and just possibly in trouble again, he's never really sure these days!

'You can walk with me if you want.' The old guy looks harmless enough, not at all threatening and Jake welcomes the bit of kindness he's offering.

'Thank you, Sir!' They start tramping along and Jake asks hesitantly, 'Where are we going?'

The older guy laughs and says, 'Good question! Me? I'm just heading west. I heard there's good fortune and plenty of jobs over in California. You know, working on the orange orchards and that. The orange industry is going through the roof these days. So, sounds like as good a plan as any.'

'Oh, OK.' He notices his voice and accent are totally at odds with his weather-beaten appearance. 'I'm Jake McMullen, sir and I'm not even sure how I got here, let alone where I'm going.'

'Hello Jake! I'm Christopher Fletcher, not *sir* and sorry but I can't help you with that. I'm not even sure how *I* got here! One minute I had a cushy job, a beautiful home, a happy and loving family and everything I could ever want from life and then, in the space of one day's trading, I lost almost everything and ended up here!' He nods towards the road.

'Almost?' Looking at the guy's predicament, how could he still think he has anything left? And what could that something be?

'I've still got my family but everything else?' He shrugs theatrically as if to say "Gone!"

Jake is taken aback by this. He'd assumed the guy must have lived like this for quite a while but it sounds like it's all been pretty recent. And Christopher is so softly spoken and sounds so well-bred that he can't believe this could have happened to him this way. He's obviously been a victim of the Crash.

He asks hesitantly, 'Sorry, Christopher but were you caught in the crash?'

'Sure was! Would you believe I was an accountant and *I* advised my clients how to invest *their* money? And what did *I* do? I invested *all* of mine in stocks and shares! A word of advice, friend, don't ever get caught up in that game! Sure, dabble a bit if you want to but only invest what you can afford to lose.'

Jake nods and mulls this over. He'd heard other people say the same thing about gambling, even the pokies but he'd always thought it was rubbish but hadn't Danny said that the stock market was just another form of gambling?

Mmm, he'll have to think more about this later on. They walk along in silence for a while, each lost in his own thoughts until Jake asks, 'Do you have any children?'

'Yes. Yes, I do.' His face clouds over with sadness. 'I have a wonderful wife, three beautiful kids and of course, the omnipresent all-American pet dog! Sally, my wife, has been a tower of strength through all of this. I've had to leave them back at her mother's house for the duration while I go looking for work but at least I know they won't starve there.' He sniffs and wipes his eyes on his sleeve.

'I'm sorry!' Jake says and really means it.

'Thanks, mate. But what about you? What's your story? Why are you here?' he gestures to their surrounds with a sweep of his hand.

'Just learning a lesson, I suppose. I've been a bit of a problem lately,' he confesses, master of the understatement, 'and my parents don't deserve that. I think it's probably time for me to start growing up!'

'Well, you'll do that here, lad. You've got no choice.' This answer has only raised a stack of questions in Jake's mind and he's about to probe a bit more into it but just at that moment, they're interrupted by an excited yell from behind them.

'Hey! This guy's got some work for us if you want it!'

Jake and Christopher look at each other, eyes shining. '*If we want it*? Is he joking? C'mon Jake, we eat tonight!' They turn on their heels and hurry back the way they'd just come.

They'd been so lost in their conversation and musings, they didn't even notice passing the farm or the *"Workers Wanted"* sign on the side of the road. The farmer had evidently been busy building a new barn for a while now but needed some extra hands for the barn raising.

The work was relatively easy with so many eager helpers and the barn comes together almost magically *and* in no time at all. With the job done, the farmer goes to each man and gives him a dollar for his help and a package of sandwiches and fruit from his wife.

She hopes the food will help them along a little bit while they're on their way in search of work. Jake can't believe that all they got was one lousy dollar for all that hard work but the other men seem to be over the moon with it; obviously $1 is worth a lot more in 1929 than it is in 2022!

The sun's setting and Jake starts getting jittery. He'd thought Danny would be here by now to bring all this to an end and boy, does he want it all to be over with! Every muscle and joint is aching from the hard, physical labour.

It hadn't seemed so bad earlier in the day when his adrenalin was still pumping and his muscles were warm and pliable but now that the twilight is setting in and he's cooling down, his muscles are tightening up and bringing the blossoming aches and pains of a day's hard labour.

And another thing, he has blisters on his blisters! If he has to spend any longer here, he doesn't know how he'll survive! But at least he did a good, hard day's work and earned his own way, along with the other men and it felt good! Here, he's not the kid who needs looking after. Here, he's a man among men!

'Jake! Are you ready to go?' Christopher calls and that's enough to send Jake scampering around to gather his things and leave the farm with his new friend.

'Do you know, that's the first dollar I've ever actually earned for myself?' he tells Christopher proudly. But the answer he gets back surprises him.

'Well, just watch out for it. Put it somewhere safe until you really need it.'

'I will,' he answers, puzzled and Christopher seeing the unasked questions on Jake's face, smiles softly and says:

'Not everyone on the road can be trusted, son. They'll either rob you blind or find another way to wangle you out of it. Just stay close to me and you'll be right.'

Jake is outraged at this, 'Not any of *these* guys, though; they all seem like really good blokes!'

Christopher smiles again at his obvious naivety and thinks, 'He'll learn!'

*

The sun has disappeared below the horizon when they finally arrive at their first "Hooverville" camp. These workers' settlements are named sarcastically after Herbert Hoover, the current President of the United States. Because of his weak relief policies, which has led to mass unemployment and the lack of a social safety net, homeless and destitute people have been forced to build these shanty towns for accommodation.

And sometimes the luckless, wandering hordes of men looking for work are lucky enough to find refuge for the night in one of them. With no vacancies here tonight though, in any of the huts, they're forced to camp out the back on the ground. The residents understand their plight and can't bring themselves to turn them away completely and the consensus between the men is it's better than the side of the road.

'There,' says Christopher, 'that looks as good a place as any for us. Just the right spot, what do you think?' Christopher leads the way over to a nice quiet niche where they'll spend the night. It's just secluded enough to make for a good night's sleep but not so far away from everybody else as to make it too welcoming to thieves and blackguards, fingers crossed.

Christopher unrolls his blanket and lays it on the ground and Jake feels like a fool. He didn't even think to bring a blanket and right at this moment, even that scummy old candlewick bedspread back there is looking pretty good.

They stake their claim and sit there, eating their sandwiches and fruit and talking about their lives so far and where they think they're heading from here. The other men all sit chatting into the night around the campfire, which is slowly dying.

Sometimes, bits and pieces of their conversations drift across to Jake and he listens, both fascinated and horrified at the same time. They're talking about the Texas and Oklahoma Panhandles and Christopher fills in the blanks for him, describing the dire situations the men are finding themselves in down there.

Thousands upon thousands of men are trekking across America looking for work, just as *they're* doing right now! Christopher tells him about the dust storms in the panhandles which are so ferocious you can't see the road ahead, with entire structures disappearing beneath thick clouds of dust.

He tries to imagine walking through that living hell, choking for air, hoping you're heading in the right direction and he feels immensely grateful for the fresh air they're breathing at the moment. He never thought he'd be so thankful for *air*!

Sooner than he expects, it's time to "hit the sack". He's put his precious dollar inside his undies as he figures if anybody tries to get it from there, they'll definitely wake him up! He tries to get comfortable on the rough, gravelly ground and surprisingly, falls straight off to sleep.

When he wakes the next morning, his stomach starts grumbling with hunger as he smells the delicious aromas of brewing coffee and frying bacon and his eyes spring open in excited anticipation. But all thought of food is banished by the sight that greets him and he's really glad that he took that precaution last night with his valuable dollar!

His belongings are scattered all over the ground and as he packs them all away, he sees that the only thing that's gone is his dime. He feels let down and betrayed, even though he doesn't even know most of these guys' names, he'd felt they were almost a team.

'Are you OK?' Christopher asks, looking at Jake's disillusioned face. 'Have you lost your dollar?'

'No, no, they didn't get that. The only thing they took was my dime, so that shows the only thing they were interested in was the money.' He looks dejectedly around and sees the men all packing up their belongings and wonders which one it was but nobody looks remotely guilty to him. Guess he'll never know. And all for ten cents!

He looks over to the campfire and realises he must have only been dreaming about the brewing coffee and frying bacon. He was sure someone was getting breakfast ready but there's none of the hustle and bustle of preparation around the campfire he was expecting to see and the fire pit is now cold and grey. What did he expect?

He's not on a school camp now, idiot! But he's not surprised he was dreaming of breakfast in the least; he's starving. His stomach growls, sounding more like a grumble than a rumble and he gladly accepts the offer to share Christopher's water with him.

He'll have to buy some provisions in the next town they come to with some of his hard-earned dollar and try to repay Christopher for his kindness.

And so they set off, traipsing along the road in a ragtag group towards what seems like absolutely nothing! Bare, dry country stretches for miles and miles as far as the eye can see. Not a hint of a homestead, not even an empty one; just rocks, bushes and dirt.

Jake remains constantly on the lookout for any signs of civilisation and Christopher feels sorrier and sorrier for him as time goes on. He's so young that his endless hope is still intact but he knows that they have many more miles of this desolate landscape to cross before they'll have any hope at all of relief.

Jake is limping, his right foot is killing him and it feels like there's something wrong with his shoe. He slips it off and shaking it out, he sees a sharp little stone fall to the ground. How did that get in there? He picks it up to take a closer look and shoves it absentmindedly in his pocket.

As he bends down to tie his shoe back on, he starts feeling dizzy from the lack of any real food and water. Not helping is the sight he'd been met with when he'd taken his shoe off. The constant walking has left his foot bleeding and numb and he's pretty sure that, if he took off the other shoe, that foot would be in the same condition. He should do something about them before they become infected but what can he do out here?

Suddenly, he hears excited voices from the front of the contingent and the men start pointing and shouting to each other. He looks ahead and in the distance, sees a train sitting dead still on a track to the side of the road. It looks as though it's waiting for something, maybe a truck or another train loaded with cargo? Jake can't think of any other reason this train would be sitting stock still as it is, in the middle of nowhere.

It turns out that when the train is heading back home after emptying its load, this particular train driver had started stopping for a while at this spot to pick up and help out any men who need a ride. As he's told his wife so many times before, 'If these guys are putting themselves through that hell to help their families, it's the least I can do. Headin' back that way anyway, so why go straight past 'em with an empty train?' And she loves him for that even more!'

The men all race straight down and after finding the doors open, they all start piling in for a "free ride" to the nearest town. Jake looks up at Christopher asking if it's alright to do that? 'I mean, what if they ask for tickets?'

He's not too happy to be doing this at all as he suspects it is totally illegal but Christopher boards the train just ahead of him and turns around, extending his hand to help Jake board. Jake picks up his bag and turns, looking up at Christopher's outstretched hand and sees Danny!

Chapter Eleven
2022-Mountview

Jake looks up into Danny's eyes and simply says, 'I'm *starving*!'

Danny laughs and looks back at him with a tinge of sympathy. Poor kid. 'Welcome back! And don't worry, that hunger's only a memory, we've not long had dinner so you're all right.'

'Dinner? What time is it?'

'Seven-thirty, you've been asleep for half an hour.'

He can't quite get his head around how he can be gone overnight but have only actually been gone half an hour or so when he gets back. He could understand nodding off and dreaming it all while Danny's talking; that wouldn't be so unusual, he always went to sleep in history at school but this is different.

He can't believe these "visions" are not real, he *knows* he was there! And because he's *living* the history, he finally gets that you *can* actually learn from it. He sits solemnly on the bed and tries to share these new experiences with Danny.

From the threatening landlord right through to the railroad carriage and tries to describe as best he can, not just *what* happened back then but *how* it felt and how that brought the differences with today into even sharper focus.

'God, it was hard. You couldn't just get another job like you can today. Everywhere and everybody was just going bust,' he starts, 'There were so many men out on the road looking for work just to feed themselves until they got to California or somewhere else where they might be lucky enough to get a proper job, so they could send money back to their families. And they were the lucky ones! Other men didn't even make it that far.'

He stops talking and hangs his head, remembering, 'Danny, I mean they really couldn't go on. I saw an ambulance racing along the street to one of the buildings and then I heard a woman say, "Another jumper!" Next thing all the people in the street were talking about it.

'I just put my head down and kept walking until I was out of there. I didn't know where I was going but I kept going anyway. And then I got really lucky! I met a guy called Christopher Fletcher and he let me walk with him. He got caught up in the crash too and ended up with nothing but he stayed with me and sort of protected me all the way.

'Even sharing his water with me because I hadn't taken any. I was an absolute idiot. I didn't even think to take a blanket, so I just had to sleep on the bare ground.'

'He sounds like a good man. You're right, you were lucky but bad times like that can definitely bring out the best in people,' Danny says but thinks to himself, 'And the worst!'

'And the worst!' Jake says out loud, simultaneously giving voice to Danny's own thought and causing Danny to wonder if he'd actually said it aloud.

However, oblivious to this cross over Jake continues, enthusiastically getting into his stride and warming up to this part of the story. He goes on to tell Danny about waking up to find his belongings thrown all over the ground and his precious dime gone. 'But luckily, I hid my dollar so they couldn't find that!'

'Your dollar? Where did that come from? How much did you have in your pocket when you left your boarding house?'

'Only that dime but then we came across this farmer who needed help with a "Barn Raising". Most of it was already done. The framework was already up but the farmer needed help with the walls and roof. Anyway, we all helped with that and up it went. I couldn't believe how quick it was!

'He gave us each a dollar for it and his wife gave us sandwiches and fruit to have as well. But you know what? I thought about it later, that was the first dollar I've ever earned for myself!'

'Good on you, mate! I bet that made you feel good!'

'It did, actually! Even though it was only *one* lousy dollar, it was *my* lousy dollar not one that I had to get off Dad!'

'I know "one lousy dollar" doesn't sound like much to you now but back in those days, a man could eat well on that. Maybe not his whole family but it would keep him going for a good, few days if he spent it right! I remember reading where those poor guys had been picking up jobs where they were lucky to earn thirty cents for a full day's work, so one dollar was like a luxury to them.'

'Yeah, they looked like they'd won the lottery, so now I know why. None of their families were there anyway and they only had themselves to feed and like you said, it would keep them going.'

'Yeah, they had to keep their strength up to make it through and find a better way forward. And another good thing was the integrity those guys had back in those days. They worked and worked hard for what they had and prided themselves on that.

'No job was too big or too small. They just grabbed what they could with both hands *whenever* they could get it. It was a real sense of *achievement* to be earning their own money and not living off charity and that's what kept them going; no matter what the conditions were like!'

'Yeah, I get that now! That's how I felt holding that dollar.'

He tells Danny just how physically hard it was to be in that position. Constantly walking all day every day and he recounts the story of the stone in his shoe! 'It was only small but felt like a bloody rock! Here, look!' He reaches into his pocket to show him just how small and sharp it is and of course, it's not there. He laughs self-consciously.

'Sometimes I still can't believe I'm not really there and it's all just a dream. You're not a hypnotist, are you?'

'A hypnotist? No way! But you know what? If you feel like you were there, then OK, you were there. Full stop! In life, always hold on to what you believe in and if it helps, just think of all the good stuff you've learned while you've been there.'

Jake thinks this sounds a bit like mixed messages to him. Danny's always said that, of course he hadn't actually been there but now he's saying if he wants it to be true, then it is! What, like Father Christmas and the Tooth Fairy? Come on, that might have worked when he was a kid but he's definitely not falling for it now.

It sounds more like a perfect way for Danny to dodge answering the question to him.

'It teaches you the value of money though, doesn't it? Not just what one dollar will buy but the value of earning that dollar yourself if you get my drift.'

'Yeah, I think I do now. I've got a lot to think about. Like what I'm going to do for the rest of my life and how I'm going to get enough of those dollars to pay for it all!'

Danny knows now that money really is the root of all evil and starts thinking back to the time when he learned that lesson the hard way.

Danny

The house has been a whirl of activity for the last week and every surface is cleaned and scrubbed to within an inch of its life. Danny looks at all the shiny, expectant faces around the breakfast table and feels the festive anticipation radiating from each one.

The Robertson's are beaming, the twins are beside themselves with excitement and Cheryl is giggling at every little thing that happens. And the reason for all this turmoil? The imminent arrival of their son and brother Paul; home at last from his year's work experience on the Fielding farm in England.

Danny's no fool and he knows things will be different from now on. Paul's back and he'll take over the farm duties that Danny had resumed now that the twins were getting ready to head off to boarding school. So, if he wants to stay, he'll have to find a job and probably somewhere else to live as well.

'Hi,' Janet Thompson smiles up at Danny as he walks into the kitchen. 'I've just been on the phone to Marjorie Chapman and she said to let you know that St Christopher's Public School in Dubbo is looking for a new teacher at the moment, if you're interested. 'But are you sure you won't stay on here with us? We can always use another pair of hands about the place, you know. Please don't feel like you have to go just because Paul's back.'

'I don't feel that at all! You've all made me feel very welcome but I think if I'm going to make my home down here, then I need to start building my own life. And besides, I want to give Cheryl and our kids the best possible future.'

'Kids?'

'Ha ha! No, I don't mean right now but definitely down the track! I think I'll go and give the school a ring but I don't like my chances.'

'We can give you a reference if you like and I'm sure Debbie from the School of the Air will vouch for you as well!'

'Thank you that would be great!' He wanders off with his mind full of the exciting possibilities ahead.

*

Two months later, Danny throws the last of his packing boxes onto the Dubbo Tip and dusts his hands off as he walks back to the car. He's been working at the school for three weeks now and is really settling into the life as a fifth-class teacher and with the last of his cartons unpacked, he's also very happy with his little two-bedroom flat.

His father had reluctantly agreed to help him with the deposit but was absolutely gutted when Danny had told him he was staying. His plans for "Crofters Estate" were all now up in the air that Danny would not be working it and stocking it with future Fieldings and that just breaks his heart.

'And what about this girl you intend to marry? What exactly is she looking for?'

'Dad! Her name is Cheryl and she's not "looking" for anything! I can't understand you; you thought enough of the Robertson's to send me here for a year but not enough to want me to marry into the family? And if you think she's after your land, let me tell you "Whitegum Station" is thousands and thousands of hectares. It makes our place look like a hobby farm!'

He is shocked at his Father's reaction but totally expected his Mother's. Her dreams of the big, society wedding all disappear down the drain and she's mortified! It seems she doesn't really care who he marries or where he lives, as long as she and Babs can plan the event; she even had her outfit planned! All of this only proves to him yet again that he's right to stay!

Cheryl stays on the farm, helping Paul to settle in and finding ways to utilise what he's learned in Hertfordshire to improve the way they do certain things here. She teases him mercilessly about his new-found English accent and marvels at the stories of the loaded morning sideboard, nightly three course dinners and extravagant parties.

Although he seems to be rather reticent when it comes to the question of girls and romance! Oh well, he needs to keep some things to himself, she thinks but she still needs to stifle a giggle every time he says that gentlemen do not do this or gentlemen do not do that.

Gentlemen? He'll be back down to earth before long, that's for sure! As captivated as she is by his stories, she misses Danny dreadfully and according to him, the feeling is mutual. Thank heavens for Saturdays and her day off!

First term ends with the kids running jubilantly through the school gates and Danny packing his bags to head back to the farm for a fortnight's visit. He's looking forward to getting into some hard work again and building his shrinking muscles back up.

The men are all glad to welcome him back, just as much as the family are and he puts in the long hours alongside them. He soon realises just how much he misses being there when they all retire to the veranda on the first night after one of Mrs Robertson's famous roast lamb dinners.

The holidays fly past and in what seems like the click of a finger, he's back in his classroom standing in front of twenty-six restless eleven-year-olds.

On the second day back, his phone rings early in the morning and he jumps up out of bed with a sick feeling in the pit of his stomach; what's wrong? Nobody would ring this early in the morning unless something had happened! He lets out a huge sigh of relief when he hears Anthony Copeland's voice on the other end of the line.

'Sorry it's so early, mate,' he croaks into the phone, 'but I just can't make it in, this bloody flu! Would you be able to fill in for me for a couple of days?'

'God, Tony, you sound dreadful! Of course, it's alright with me as long as it's OK with the boss. I'll check our classes and see how I can wrangle it.'

'Thanks, mate! I know you'll work it all out. Talk to you later.' And with that he hangs up and Danny is left looking at the phone wondering why he'd called him directly and not the headmaster as would have been the correct procedure. He shrugs and decides that as he's up now, he may as well get ready and go in early to get it all organised.

Bill, the headmaster, frowns when Danny relays the details of his early morning call.

Why the hell didn't he ring him? Danny is great but not as experienced as some of the others.

His first impulse is to say no but he's already looking excited by the idea and has come to him prepared with ideas for how he can balance the two and actually combine some of the lessons. So, he decides to let him have a go.

The time passes quickly enough and the kids all seem happy with the arrangement, taking easily to Danny's soft but firm approach, something he learned from Mr Robertson.

So, Bill is especially upset to have to approach Danny with this matter but knows he has to.

Anthony has been in charge of the school's Charity Fundraising Programme and always has a cash float of $5,000 in his care to fund any future fundraisers *the school might want to be involved in. With his flu finally a thing of the past, he walks into Bill's office one morning, his wrinkled face etched with worry.*

The money is gone! The whole $5,000! He doesn't want to point the finger at anyone but the only person who had access to the safe was Danny and the deposit/withdrawal book he kept in there with the cash had been fiddled with as if there'd been a withdrawal!

Bill can't believe that Danny would do something like this, he's always thought what a good bloke he is. But then, he's only known him for a couple of months and he's known Anthony for years and he definitely knows that he would never steal from the school or the local charities! There's only one thing for it and that is to confront Danny with the facts and try to gauge his reaction.

Danny is gobsmacked as the realisation that he's being accused of stealing the money slowly sinks in.

'Why would I do that?'

'Well, you have been telling everybody that you're struggling to save for your wedding.' Bill shrugs, 'Have you any idea where this money could be? Did you leave the keys lying around at any time? I'll be honest with you, I'm having trouble accepting any of this. I never would have thought it of you.'

Danny's problems only become worse when Bill calls the police because Danny won't admit that he's done it. Bill has told him if he replaces the money, he'll let it go and put it down to a big mistake. But Danny keeps proclaiming his innocence and so he's charged with both theft and fraud.

He still thinks it's all a misunderstanding and somebody will come forward with the true story to prove he didn't do it. But nothing like that happens.

He's devastated when the Robertson's don't appear in court to speak on his behalf. He can't understand how they could have any doubts about him and actually wishes he would have gone home at the end of his apprenticeship.

With his defence not having much to pin his hopes to, he's found guilty and sentenced to five years in a low security Sydney jail.

'We'll appeal,' his solicitor tells him and they do but to no avail. Danny is now a guest of Her Majesty for the next five years.

*

Danny tells Jake an abridged version of this part of his story, highlighting his quest for a teaching job and the enormous satisfaction he derived from that role including the sense of achievement he felt whenever saw the penny drop for a struggling student.

'It was the same feeling you had when you helped with the barn raising. A real sense that, sure it was hard work but just look at what you helped to build!'

'Yeah, I know what you mean now. It doesn't matter how many times people tell you about it, you can't really understand it until you feel it for yourself.'

Danny watches Jake looking down at the floor deep in thought and figures there would be nothing to gain for either of them to tell him the whole sorry story of the missing money and how he'd ended up in here.

Meanwhile, Jake's mind is a riot of memories, feelings and speculations. He needs to get it all sorted and diarised right now, so he pulls his diary out. Danny takes this as a sign that the conversation has come to an end. He sits back, picks up his own book and gives Jake some space to write in peace.

*

Dear Diary

Day Three, Wednesday.

Tonight, I spent a day in New York! I was in the 1929 Great Depression, right after the Wall St Crash and the place was in total chaos. I had to run away late at night because an angry landlord was banging on my door, reckoned I hadn't paid my rent and the streets were really full and busy even then at that time of the night.

But I did get away from there, thank heavens and I teamed up with a man called Christopher to go looking for work. Yes, ME looking for work! Ha! I should look him up when I get home and see if I can find out what happened to him, then I'll see if it was real or just my *imagination*, as Danny keeps telling me!

We walked and talked for a long way and then we came to a farm where they needed some extra muscle to finish building a barn. We all worked there the rest of that day and I couldn't believe it when he only gave us one lousy dollar each!

I was pretty miffed until Danny told me just what you could buy with that dollar in those days and it's a lot more than you can today! Then it dawned on me that it was actually my dollar, I earned it, the first one I've ever earned for myself in my life!

I owned it free and clear without feeling guilty or obliged to Dad for every cent. I wish I still could have had it when I got back, I'd frame it and put it on my bedroom wall.

Guilty to Dad for money? When did I start feeling guilty about that? I suppose it must have been in the back of my mind all along and this sort of thing brought it to the front. Could be why I'm so resentful all the time. Yeah, resentful.

I sort of do resent him just dishing out whatever I ask for, because then he keeps me feeling like I owe him! Maybe that's why he treats me like I'm still a kid but the men on the road treated me like I was one of them and part of the team.

And it was strange but just the fact that I earned my own money made me feel like I was on the same level as them anyway; an adult, not a little kid who needed looking after.

But even more than that, I had this funny feeling looking at the barn I'd helped build. I felt proud that I'd been part of it, it just looked so solid and well built, like it had always been there. I wonder if it's still there today. Yeah, there's a heap of good stuff about working that I hadn't even thought about before. Whenever I get out of here, I am going to get a job; if anyone'll have me, that is.

I keep wondering what happened to all those guys. Having to just pack up and go, leaving their homes and families. It must have been really hard, none of them even knew if they'd ever see them again. I'd like to be able to find out where they all ended up.

They could have stayed in New York and taken handouts and charity but all of them were in the same boat and they didn't want to do that, they wanted to earn their own money so they could support their families and nothing was going to stand in their way!

I'm not going to forget all this when I get home. I'm going to make big changes and start working my way up to build a future for myself. But I'll start planning exactly how I'm going to do that in the morning, I'm bushed!

Goodnight, Diary!

*

He slams the diary shut with such a look of determination on his face that Danny looks up from his reading, eyebrows shooting up and thinks, 'Good!'

Jake changes for bed and hops in thinking that whether these "adventures" are as real as they feel or exactly what Danny says they are, all in his mind, he doesn't want them to stop. He's getting a lot from them.

But he decides, he'd better keep an open mind on just how real or imaginary they are until he goes to the showers the next morning and there, securely hidden in his underpants, is an American dollar!

Chapter Twelve
Thursday-Mountview

Sitting on the couch in the TV room, Jake is fully involved in his murder mystery as the climax builds and the edge of the seat action becomes positively nail-biting. He is so totally involved in the story that he doesn't even notice Ernie come in and take his usual spot on the other end of the couch.

Ernie looks over at him and smiles, thinking that he looks like a school kid today, his head still buried in the pages and oblivious to everything going on around him. He has a fair idea who the culprit is but who knows what twists and turns await him through the final chapters? He'll just have to keep reading and find out and he's determined to do that today.

At least breakfast was vastly improved this morning and for that Jake is very thankful, especially after the last couple of days of bodge-it-up and dish-it-out fare. Ernie is staring blindly at the silent television. He's actually turned the sound completely off and is just watching the colourful, moving figures in mime.

'How can you watch it like that?' Jake asks, 'Don't you want to know what they're saying?'

'Nah mate. Don't bother me one bit. Couldn' care less what they're sayin' anymore! I gave up watchin' it years ago in the mornin's, after all 'ow many ads for vacuum cleaners and vegetable choppers can ya watch?'

He asks what Jake's been up to and Jake outlines his dreams, self-consciously admitting that at the end of each one he keeps thinking that they're real and that he was actually there living through it all. But he always feels like a fool the next morning when Danny tells him that they're not and he hasn't left the cell.

'I mean, of course I hadn't. How could I?'

'So, Danny's still givin' the 'istory lessons, is he?' Ernie's face softens with the memories, 'Know what ya mean, though. I still 'aven't worked out if they was real or not. He's a bloody good storyteller at any rate.'

'I know. I was sort of thinking that's all there was to it as well but then something else happened and it made me think again.' He leaves it at that and goes back to his book, leaving Ernie sitting quietly wondering what happened for him to make him think like that.

But with Jake once again engrossed and knee deep in his murder mystery, he goes back to staring at the screen, leaving his questions unanswered.

A young guy wanders in and goes straight to the ping pong table at the back of the room. Several other guys are having a hit and cheering each other on and the newcomer asks if he can join them.

'This table isn't for *your* kind, mate! Why don't ya just go back to the jungle?'

Jake jumps up at this and walks slowly over, extending his hand as he reaches the boy. 'Hi, mate! I'm Jake,' he says loudly as he firmly shakes hands with him. 'Let me know when the table's available and we'll have a game, eh?'

'Sounds like a plan!' Huge white teeth shine from rich, glowing ebony skin. 'I'm Shane.'

'Bloody do-gooders!' the leader of the pack spits out. 'C'mon, let's get out of here! I can't stand the bloody stench!' The others meekly follow his lead and heads bowed, they follow him out of the room.

'Don't worry about them; if they had half a brain, they'd be dangerous! So, we're right!' Jake laughs as he picks up a discarded bat. 'Where are ya from?'

'Kenya and I am so used to ignorant taunts like these that they just roll off my back! But thanks for that. Let's have a game.'

They pick up the ball and Shane serves to Jake, which he misses by a mile and has to chase the escapee ball around the floor. 'Looks like I jumped in too soon. I forgot that I can't play to save myself!'

Shane laughs with a rich throaty appreciation. 'That's alright. I'll give you some pointers.'

Shane and Jake continue on for the next hour and by the end of it, Jake can at least hit the ball back but he knows he's not giving Shane the game he deserves.

Ernie sits quietly, listening to the interaction between the two boys as they play and wonders if Jake would have even thought about doing that before he came in here or how much of it has been born through Danny's influence.

When a couple of other guys walk in and eye off the table, the boys immediately hand their bats over, "share and share alike" is one of his mother's favourite mantras. Except he just never worked out exactly what he was supposed to share with Chelsea except the dreaded bathroom, of course.

He smiles up at Shane thinking that he must be six-five or six-six. He feels like a kid next to him. 'Thanks for that. Think I'm going to need a lot more practice, though!'

'My pleasure. Want to give it another go tomorrow?'

'Yep, sure do. Same bat-time, same bat-table?' They both laugh and Shane wanders out to the exercise yard while Jake heads back to finish solving the mystery of the Outback Murders.

He hadn't even bothered looking for Danny today, he knows that he'll never find him anyway or the library for that matter and it's not worth his time and effort even trying. He does wonder fleetingly why he has to be at work so early every day though.

What can he have to do in there that's so important he has to be in there at daybreak every day of the week? Guess nothing in here is like it is on the outside.

So, he sits back down with Ernie in companionable silence, only broken by turning the pages of his book. He's found he really likes this quiet time in here after breakfast. The others are all outside and their angry raised voices can be heard occasionally fighting and arguing.

Sometimes, he watches these skirmishes through the window whenever they take place with an almost morbid curiosity. Although it does make him feel like he's spying on them, watching from inside behind the barred windows all safe and sound, while he leaves it to them to battle it out in the exercise yard like a bunch of warring schoolboys in a playground.

But about an hour later, while he's doing just that and standing there at the window agog at the latest brawl, he hears his name being called loudly behind him! He jumps, what's he done now? And turns slowly to face the guard who's standing there with a sheet of paper in his hand.

'Where's everybody else?'

'Outside, Sir.'

'Yeah, they would be, wouldn't they? OK, come with me and I'll round 'em up.'

'Yes, Sir!' What he is rounding us up for, he wonders. Might be getting a work team together to do some yard work or something like that. That's OK. He moves to follow the guard through the door and looks at Ernie, his worry obvious on his face.

But his old mate smiles and whispers to him on the way out, 'You've got a visitor, son!' Oh, of course! Jake smiles his relief and his thanks and quickly follows the guard out before he really is in trouble.

When they have everybody on the list together, they all traipse in single file to the visitors' room.

*

His mother is sitting at a different table today but that's the only thing that's different. She's still alone and waiting patiently for him to join her. Still hanging her head and still cradling her hands in her lap. Being a mother, she has been worried sick every day and unable to sleep at all every night and the constant stress is really starting to show on her gently lined face.

Lost in her thoughts, she doesn't even notice him approach the table so when he plonks down heavily on the seat opposite her a few moments later, she jerks her head up in surprise.

'Oh, hello darling! How are you?'

'Hi, Mum! Actually, I'm pretty good, thanks!' He smiles widely and takes hold of her hand. 'You've got to stop worrying about me!'

Diana looks at her son and forces herself to really take him in, every detail and she's stunned by what she sees. He hasn't looked so well, so healthy or so happy in ages. The haunted eyes and drawn face have all gone and instead she sees a confident young man in his place.

Maybe Geoffrey is right, maybe this isn't such a bad place for him to be for a *short* while. Her only worry now is where he'll be sent if he does get prison time as a part of his sentence. She tells him that Kenny has woken up and looks like he's going to be fine!

But even though she's still so angry she can barely stand to look at him, she was absolutely mortified to hear that the second he came round, the police were waiting right there at his bedside for heaven's sake and immediately charged him with all the same offences as Jake's facing. Couldn't they wait until he was better?

He'd only just opened his eyes! He was currently under police watch in the hospital until he's well enough to face the court. She'd gone home fretting that she couldn't believe they'd treat these children this way. But of course, Geoffrey had only told her to pull herself together. They were eighteen, not children anymore and they'd committed some pretty serious crimes that night. They will just have to face what they've got coming to them and work the rest of their lives out after that.

She'd gone through most of this, only holding back his father's reaction, after Jake had asked if she'd heard how Kenny was getting on. Of course, he's immensely relieved that he's going to be OK but he tells his Mum he also feels really guilty for egging him on to steal the car in the first place.

Look what he got them into. Big men! He hopes it all goes well for him at least, maybe he should talk to his solicitor and point out that it was all his idea.

Maybe that might help Kenny a bit. He can only try.

'And how's your flatmate, Danny, going?' Diana asks, feeling that she needs to change the subject but surprised and proud that Jake has accepted his role in the fiasco and Kenny's part in it as well. Yes, he's definitely changing, finally growing up and starting to act like it. What are they feeding him in here?

'He's a *cell*mate, Mum, not a *flat*mate!'

Diana fidgets and fusses, 'Yes, yes, of course he is.'

'And he's great, thanks. I'll let him know you asked. Mum, he never gets any visitors and never mentions hearing from any family or anything. I think he might be on his own out here.'

'Out here? Where's he from?'

'He grew up in England, so maybe all his family and that are back over there, I don't know.'

'Yes, that's probably it. Have you had any more history lessons from him?'

'Boy, have I! Last night we were talking about the Wall St Crash and the Great Depression. You wouldn't believe what it was like back then!'

'I do have some idea, Jake!' Her kids never fail to amaze her. They both think she and Geoffrey came down in the last shower. 'After all I haven't been living under a rock, you know.'

'Yeah, sorry Mum.' They go on to have quite a conversation about the itinerant workers, the suicides and the families who'd all been split apart before they've exhausted that topic and she looks over to him with a smile. 'Well, you've certainly been brushing up on your history if nothing else! But on a different note, I *have* got some good news for you.

'I'm definitely making some headway with your father! He seems to be softening up a bit on the subject of your bail. But I'll keep working on him, you know what good old Churchill said, "never surrender!" Maybe by the end of the week, I'll have some even better news for you. Fingers crossed.'

When she's gone, Jake heads back to the TV room and sits staring at his feet not seeing what's on the telly or caring either for that matter. *Blasted money*! Why does everything always come back to *money*? He thinks that it'll be good to talk to Danny about this tonight and get his thoughts on it.

*

'You're in a good mood!' Danny says as Jake comes into their cell and sits on the bed facing him with a big smile on his face. 'What's happened to put that smile on your face, then?'

'I had a visit from Mum today and you'll never guess what; she thinks Dad's coming around to the idea of the bail!'

'Great. All you need is the money.'

'Yeah, I know. I was thinking about that too. I've always just thought of it as Dad having a never-ending supply to give me whenever I put my hand out. But I never thought what would happen if he didn't just give it to me, especially when I might actually *need* it more than anything else in the world, like now or like last night as well!

'I mean, back then I was panicking so much that I might lose *one dollar* that I actually had to hide it. I needed it for food, water, survival—plain and simple and that was bad enough but just look what happened to Christopher and his family. He lost all of his and he had to leave them behind for God knows how long. Yeah, we both needed it then and now I need it again to get out of here.'

'Yeah, you're right! But also, don't forget about old Ambrose Ross. How he used and abused his wealth was nothing short of criminal!'

'What do you mean abused?'

'Well, just think about it. All the world's most powerful men are all filthy rich, aren't they? Some of them use their wealth and power to do good things and help people. But then there are others like "Master Ross" who used that power to bully people and wreak havoc. Just like he treated you! It was like in his eyes he bought you and therefore, he owned you and because of that, he had all the power over you!'

'Yeah, he thought he could treat people however he wanted and not have to answer to anybody for it.' Jake thinks about this for a while and finally adds, 'You know, it'd probably be a pretty dangerous thing, having that much power in the wrong hands, don't you think?'

'I certainly do! And again, you see examples of that all through history. From the start of time, people wanted to have the power, whether it was money or territory that gave it to them and usually there was nothing they wouldn't do to get it. And that's right up to today!'

'No wonder there's been so many wars then!'

'Exactly! Just look at World War II. The year before war broke out, the troubles had already been brewing. Can you believe one man had the power and he alone decided that people of different religions and races were unacceptable in *his* country and that man was?'

'Adolph Hitler?'

'Adolph Hitler, of course! He'd decided that he wanted a pure-bred Aryan race, so he simply made the decision to rid Germany of anybody who was, in his view, tainted. Then one night he saw a prime opportunity to start the ball rolling, as they say, with the assassination of a diplomat named Ernst vom Rath. And what followed his death on that dreadful night became known as "Kristallnacht".'

'Kristallnacht?' Jake tries the word out, rolling it around on his tongue.

'It means "Crystal Night" or "The Night of Broken Glass".' Danny looks at Jake thoughtfully and just says, 'This one's a hard one to put into words.'

Chapter Thirteen
9 November 1938-Germany

It looks to be late at night in a dark, deserted street. Jake's not sure where he is but he knows for sure it's not Australia and he thanks his lucky stars that Danny has stayed with him this time. The village he finds himself in has a quaint, old-world feel that makes him think of the old fairy tales his mother used to read to him when he was a little boy.

He almost expects it to start snowing! Disembodied voices drift over to them, echoing in the crisp, clear night air and he turns to Danny, whispering, 'Where are we?'

'We're in Germany just before World War 2. And why are you whispering?'

'I don't know. It's just so quiet here!' Jake shrugs. He can't find the right words to explain the mood he feels in this deserted street so "quiet" will have to do. They walk over to the park and sit on a bench just a little way away from a neighbouring seat where two men are in deep discussion, their heads bent low towards each other.

They're not as reticent as Jake to disturb the slumbering silence of the night but they're still keeping their voices relatively low but luckily just loud enough for the boys to hear quite clearly what they're talking about. Jake listens intently to what seems to be a history lesson unfolding right before him.

'You're right! Ever since Ernst vom Rath was shot down in cold blood on Monday, something's been brewing.'

'Yes, that was terrible. And so brazen. They say it was a student!'

'A Polish-Jewish student, of course!' the first man added ominously. 'Herschel Grynszpan. They say the news travelled quickly to Hitler in Munich and you know how volatile he can be!'

'He'd be in the mood for trouble too. He's not going to like losing vom Rath.'

'No! Mark my words, there's going to be big trouble for his death. It's just what Hitler's been waiting for!'

'I think you're right but I do keep a small hope we're wrong! If they've already arrested that boy, what good could come of more trouble? What can he hope to *achieve* from any more fighting?'

Jake thinks it's strange the men should be talking in such heavily accented English.

He thinks German must be their first language but maybe they thought he and Danny were German and wouldn't understand what they were saying?

'Well, we'll just have to wait and see but for now, I'm getting home. This sort of talk in public is just plain dangerous!'

'Yes, as usual you are right, my friend and you know what they say, "the trees have ears"!'

'It's "walls" but I agree. What have we come to when we can't even talk to a friend safely under the stars in such a beautiful park as this?'

'Gute Nacht, Gunther.'

'Gute Nacht, mein Freund!'

The two men walk off in opposite directions, hands buried deep in their coat pockets and heads down trying to shrink into their clothes in order to make themselves as invisible and non-threatening as possible.

Danny speaks first when he's sure they're out of earshot. 'They're right, you know. There's definitely trouble brewing and—'

BANG!

CRASH!

The boys jump in fright and look towards the source of the disturbance. Their surprise is quickly replaced by horror when they see the "Brown Shirts" of the Nazi Party militia storming their way down the street, smashing and burning anything in their path.

'They're just smashing *anything*!' Jake cries in terror.

'Yeah, anything they believe belongs to a Jew!' Danny points out before grabbing Jake and trying to make a run for it to find them both a safe hiding spot. Minutes later, as well concealed as possible, they sit silently watching the carnage play out in front of their eyes.

Not only shops and homes are being targeted but Jake feels sick to his stomach when he sees them destroying a synagogue, emptying it of anything valuable first of course and then burning the sacred building to the ground!

Shop fronts and windows are being smashed at will and any person who's silly or brave enough to try to impede or stop them is bashed to the ground; some are simply killed where they stand. Jake starts shaking uncontrollably. The sight of this is as mesmerising as it is sickening.

Bodies lay amongst the piles of smashed glass, which nearly cover the road. Shards of broken glass shine and twinkle in the light of the fires like a macabre travesty of a festive celebration and Jake immediately understands the reference to the name given to this devastating pogrom.

He would later learn that after 2 days of this constant terror, 1000 synagogues would have been burnt to the ground, 7500 businesses would be ransacked and destroyed and 91 Jewish people would have lost their lives. How many more were injured would probably never be known.

Jewish hospitals, homes, schools and even cemeteries couldn't escape the frenzied attacks either and were also in the midst of being vandalised mercilessly across the cities that were currently under attack.

'I get it!' Jake exclaims, 'I understand now that they called it Kristallnacht because of all that broken glass.'

Danny agrees and takes it one step further pointing out that, 'It didn't stop with this one night either. They thought tonight was so successful and they were on such a high, that they thought why stop here? Can you believe, the things that followed were even more disgusting, *evil* in its purest form?'

'Do you mean the Holocaust?'

'Yep. Millions of innocent lives lost before the end of the war. Jake?' He's looking at his little mate, who seems to be so lost between the scene before them and his own thoughts, he looks positively comatose and realises he hasn't heard one word of what he's just said to him!

He's dead right too, as Jake is so busy thinking about the dreadful days they were all about to live through, he's overcome by a yearning to change things and warn them about the impending disaster waiting to unfold.

'Can't we do something to stop it?'

'Not our job. For now, you can only look and learn.'

Jake turns back to the spectacle and watches in horror as he sees several brave men try to stop the rioting blood-thirsty mob, only to be cut down ruthlessly for their efforts. He watches as other people are grabbed roughly from where they're sheltering inside buildings only to be brought out into the fray and dealt with.

And not just men either! Women and children are no safer for their gender or their age and he's really starting to get angry! He knows these scenes anger Danny just as much but unfortunately, they both also know they don't stand a chance of helping them and they both feel so powerless.

'Why? How? Where are the police?' Jake doesn't understand any of this. 'Isn't anybody going to do anything for these people?'

Danny is about to answer when they feel themselves being pushed and pulled in an aggressive show of strength from behind and dragged stumbling out to the street.

'Wie heiBen sie?' commands a soldier looking them over with an arrogant sneer.

'What?' asks Jake, confused.

'He wants to know who we are, our names.' Danny turns to the soldier and says, 'Wir sind Danny und Jake.'

'Danny? Und Jake?' The soldier pulls a face to imply "ridiculous, they're not *real* names!"

Jake pipes up, wanting to help and says, 'we're from Australia, Daniel and Jacob!' pointing in turn to both Danny and himself to illustrate that they're the owners of the names.

'*Jacob*? Der *Jude*!' And without further ado, he lifts his rifle and points it straight at Jake's forehead!

Jake immediately puts his arms up defensively and screams and suddenly the soldier is shooting into the empty space where Jake had just been standing!

Chapter Fourteen
2022-Mountview

'Are you OK?' Danny is sitting next to Jake on the floor of the cell, their backs against Jake's bed and both quite stunned at the speed in which those events had just escalated. One minute they were discussing the history, the whys and wherefores and the next thing, a member of Hitler's militia had a rifle at Jake's head and was squeezing the trigger!

'I think so,' Jake says quietly. 'He was going to shoot me!' He puts his hand up to his forehead as if to check that he really hadn't been shot. No pain, no blood. He exhales and relaxes, dropping his head back onto the mattress and staring at the ceiling. 'And for nothing!'

'That was never going to happen, I wouldn't let it! But you're right, it did happen to many others that night and unfortunately, we could only watch. If we're privileged enough to have a front seat to history unfolding, then we respect that and watch it quietly.

'If he had succeeded in killing you that would have upset the balance of everything that happened after that. We're not there to change anything, just to learn; the results of even the slightest change could be disastrous further down the line.'

Jake doesn't even begin to understand what that all means but just assumes that if Danny says it, then it must be true.

Danny stands, dusts himself off and moves over to his own bed, propping himself up in the corner and looking thoughtfully down at Jake. He's still sitting there on the ground as still and as quiet as a statue, his face the deathly white pallor of milky alabaster.

He leaves him to contemplate what's just happened and thinks that young Jake seems to be toughening up a bit. The boy who came in here bragging about his car thieving and house breaking would definitely have fainted at having a gun thrust against his forehead. And granted, he was badly shaken up but here he is now sitting deep in thought processing it all as a way of dealing with it.

Eventually, Jake pulls himself up onto the bed and rubbing his stiff neck, looks over to Danny as if something profoundly enlightening has just occurred to him but what sprouts out of his mouth is not what Danny expected at all!

'Wow, what a night! Unbelievable!'

'It sure was.'

'It's like they were all on a high! They were just *loving* it! And nobody seemed to be doing anything about it. Where were the police?'

'Nobody was going to cross Hitler or his henchmen not even the police. Or they would have been given the same treatment. You know, when Hermann Goring heard of the attacks the next day and the arrest of Herschel Grynszpan, do you know what his reaction was?' Jake shakes his head.

'He just shrugged his shoulders and said "The swine won't commit another murder. Incidentally, I wouldn't like to be a Jew in Germany!" He probably thought that was funny!'

'The swine won't commit another murder,' Jake muses, 'So was he executed?'

'I would say so. And without much preamble either, I bet. Because not only did he assassinate one of Hitler's henchmen but primarily because he was Jewish.'

'God, the racism! That guy yelled "Jude" in my face as he was lifting his rifle up to shoot me! No fair trials or innocent until proven guilty back then. Did he think I was Jewish? Was it my name? Is that why he was going to kill me?'

'I would say so.'

'But why? I hadn't done anything to him. Why did they hate the Jews so much? I just don't get it.'

'Well don't forget, Hitler wanted a pure-bred Aryan race so he was getting rid of any other religions or bloodlines that might threaten that ambition. That's why whole families were wiped out. Mothers, fathers, children. 'Grandchildren, even cousins and distant relatives that might have inherited any of that blood from their ancestors. He was a crazed maniac and nobody was safe. He thought his new race was going to breed super humans!'

'Yeah, right!' Jake scoffs, 'So that was when the Holocaust began, was it? And why?'

'I'm not a hundred percent sure, I think it might have already started before that, only a bit more low-key. Kristallnacht definitely gave him the perfect excuse to ramp it up. He considered it a real success and he felt more empowered to start throwing his weight around from that night on.'

'Bloody *bully*! That's all he was!'

'No, that wasn't all but I think bullying was a big part of his makeup.'

'I just can't get it all out of my mind, the smashing and robbing and burning and killing; it was like a feeding frenzy! They probably went on congratulating each other for weeks after that.'

'Yah and that night was only supposed to look like a "random demonstration" but it turned out to be the beginning of what they called "the pogroms" that went right through Germany and into Austria. They cleared out whole villages the same way, killing people mercilessly as they went.

'Joseph Goebbels was the Minister for Propaganda, if you can believe this thuggery was considered propaganda! He started and controlled the whole thing.'

Jake looks utterly disgusted. 'You said that was just the beginning; what happened after that?'

'Well, the pogroms happened, as I just said but also, he knew he'd sent the message loud and clear of what would happen if they tried to protest again. So, he was confident they'd squashed any opposition and they were safe to start banning Jews from schools a week later on November 15.

'Next thing they put in strict curfews a couple of weeks after that and by that December, Jews were banned from most public places in Germany. All of that happened within say, a month or so! And soon all the Jews in Germany were almost eradicated.'

'I've really got to get my head around all this. I was lucky back there but for millions of others there was no escape, was there?'

'Nope, none. But that's enough of all that. I'll just give you some space and leave you to it!' Danny picks up his book and starts reading while Jake picks up his diary, stares at the next page; a blank canvas for all his hectic thoughts and starts to write.

*

Day Four and tonight, I nearly died.

And it was racism and bigotry that nearly killed me and one bully's need for power.

We were in Germany in 1938 and it was "Crystal Night" or Danny says it's also called the "Night of Broken Glass".

Storm troopers were everywhere, smashing shops and temples and burning them down to the ground! All because this nut wanted *his* Germany to be pure bred or something!

Like he owned it! He hated all the Jews and wanted to wipe them out so badly that one guy nearly shot me because my name sounded Jewish! I don't think I've ever been so scared in my life. Thank heavens that doesn't happen in today's world or does it?

Because watching them do that to all those people made me think. They were just bullies, plain and simple, only armed and surrounded by more bullies! I've seen kids like that at school every day, really brave when they're in a group but get them on their own and they're weak as water! And there was no-one to stand up to them!

Nobody took their side! So, I suppose that's still the same today. Everybody's too scared to get involved even while the bullies are treating their victims and their stuff like garbage. Nobody deserves that! At least with everything I've done in the past, I've never been one to stand by and watch a smaller kid being picked on! I always treat people with respect and always will.

Oh. I just read over that and I think I've been kidding myself. I didn't treat Mr Peasey with respect, did I? And I certainly didn't treat his home and car with respect either. I feel like I'm really seeing myself for the first time in years in here. And I don't like what I'm seeing.

Mr Peasey was so proud of his new car and why shouldn't he be? He must have felt just as gutted as those people did when their homes and businesses were wrecked. And just like the Nazis being on a high with their "victory", didn't I do the same thing gloating over Mr Peasey's face in the rear view mirror?

I was the bully!

I feel sick.

That's it. I can't think about it anymore tonight! Jake.

Jake.

Chapter Fifteen
Friday-Mountview

'So, it was the daughter in the end,' he tells Ernie the next morning. 'You know the only books I've read before are the ones they make you read at school? So, this is the first one I read that *I* picked out and I liked it.' He walks over to the bookshelf and stands looking at what's there.

He hadn't wanted that one to end so now he feels game enough to try another one. Maybe Danny's rubbing off on him. Whatever the reason, he's sure that Miss Mitchell, his English teacher, would be proud of him.

He scans the shelves to find a title that grabs him and as he sees one that looks like it might be interesting, he reads all about it on the cover and then either keeps hold of it or puts it straight back on the shelf. He smiles when he finds one by the same author *and* it even features the same detective!

He turns to show Ernie but he's not there. He must have decided to get some fresh air and that thought appeals to Jake as well, he's hardly set foot in the yard since he arrived. He takes his book up to his cell and stashes it under his pillow before heading out.

'As Danny would say, first things first, young Jake,' He mumbles to himself as he heads back down the stairs.

He walks outside looking up at the misty, grey clouds and takes a deep lungful of the fresh spring air. That feels great! Looks like it's a pretty dreary day though but Jake can feel in his bones that it's not going to rain and even if it does, so what? It's still better than the TV room.

He scans the yard looking for either Ernie or Shane but can't pick them out in the milling groups until a loud commotion catches his attention. What's going on? He sees a large group of boys huddled together on the far left of the yard, yelling insults and raining blows down onto some poor, innocent sod in the middle of the braying, violent pack. They've worked themselves up into the same kind of frenzy he'd witnessed last night. Jake frowns.

'Monkey-see, monkey-do!'

'Went a bit crazy with the fake tan, didn't ya?'

'Answer me! Can't ya even speak English?'

'Can't speak at all, if ya ask me!'

They're all laughing and without words, egging each other on; each one trying to out-bully the last. Suddenly Jake catches a glimpse of the poor cowering, battered guy in the middle of it all and his breath catches in shock, it's Shane!

That's *it*, he thinks, this has *got* to stop! He pushes his hands deep into his pockets and saunters over, trying to look as unconcerned as possible but with butterflies of terror doing cartwheels in his stomach.

'You OK there, Shane?' All heads turn to him as one and all with the same ugly, threatening expressions distorting their faces. 'C'mon mate, something I want to show you.'

They all stand back, stunned and confused by the sheer arrogance of this wimpy kid walking straight up to *them!* Who the *hell* does he think he *is*? But Jake just walks slowly over to Shane, careful not to make any eye contact with his attackers and puts an arm around Shane's back, trying to usher him away.

But they're not ready to let him go that easily and they start moving towards them both in an aggressive column of testosterone. Jake raises his hands defensively as Shane tries to push him away. Their fight is with *him*, not Jake and he'll take whatever they're going to dish out until they get bored with him and move on but he doesn't want his friend copping a beating too for no good reason.

'It's not for no reason, mate. You're the reason! Don't you get it?'

The advancing mob descends on them and from the corner of his eye, Jake sees a couple of guards making their way over. 'Here comes the cavalry,' he thinks but still braces for the inevitable first blow when suddenly a voice rings out loud and clear.

'What's goin' on 'ere? Jake? Ya right, mate?'

'Yeah, Ernie. I'm alright.'

'Good.' He turns to their attackers, 'And *that's* the way he'll *stay*, if yas know what's good for yas! I've been dealin' with the likes of you all me life and look where it landed me.

'But you weasels know somethin'? I'm in 'ere for life, so I ain't got *nothin'* to lose. Think on that.' Jake's mouth drops open. Life? He looks up at his friend in a new light and hopes he never has cause to cross him.

The guards stop and take a step backwards seeing Ernie has everything under control and turning their back to the scene, head back to their doorway with a "Let them fight it out for themselves" attitude. They've learned not to cross Ernie when he's dealing with a problem. If he's involved, it's as good as sorted.

Jake watches them calmly accept Ernie's authority and senses their acceptance of his involvement and then he looks back at Ernie with awe. How long has he been in here already? He didn't think it was that long but he sure pulls some weight around here.

He follows Ernie's eye and sees the mob wandering off, sulking. One or two even turn back and brave throwing a contemptuous sneer Ernie's way before others in the group grab them by the arm and pull them away. Jake watches this, fascinated and noticing, not for the first time, that guys like this always roam in packs; big men in numbers but on their own, they're just a bunch of yellow-bellied cowards, still just the same as last night.

He follows their progress right to the perimeter fence where half of them squat near a rogue clump of grass that's broken its way through the concrete slab and the others just stand around doing their best Brando impersonations. They think they inspire fear but for Jake they only inspire contempt, they look ridiculous.

He bites the inside of his lip as he tries to keep a poker face and not let that contempt show through because, even though they act like trained monkeys themselves, what they were doing to Shane was way past contempt, only coming to rest somewhere around pure hatred. He's in a real bloody mess!

'You guys really alright?' Ernie asks, frowning at the blood pouring out of Shane's forehead, which is now mingling with a red stream flowing freely from his lip.

'Yeah, thanks Ernie! You're a lifesaver,' Jake mumbles as he crouches down to the trembling figure of his new friend. Ernie nods his head and walks slowly away but Jake doesn't even notice he's gone. His attention is now firmly on Shane and he sits with him quietly until his shaking and bleeding starts to subside.

'What happened?'

Shane shrugs, 'I walked out here and they just started in on me. One of them called me "Little Black Boyo" and then another one asked if my parents lived in trees. *Nobody* says that about *my* Mum!' He looks shamefacedly at Jake, 'I know I shouldn't have but I hit him. I'm not normally like that but I just saw red and I couldn't stop myself. It was a really stupid thing to do and it was more than enough to start them off. Next thing I know, they're bashing into me and calling out Monkey-see, Monkey-do.'

'Yeah, that's where I came in.'

'Trouble is I can't defend myself, I'm just not big enough.' He sees the way Jake looks at him and goes on. 'Yeah, yeah, I know I'm tall but I'm not big in other ways and I'm not a fighter. I just don't have it in me.'

'How tall are you? Six-five? Six-six?'

'Six eleven!' Jake gasps. 'But just look at the rest of me. Mum says I look like a drainpipe; yeah, she's probably right. Who knows, that could be a good job for me when I ever get out of here.'

They share a weak smile at that and then Jake tells him, 'Don't worry, you did the right thing. They were the ones who bullied you into throwing the first punch just so they could beat the hell out of you!'

'Yeah, you're prob'ly right. Anyway, looks like they've given up on it now.'

'*For* now, don't ya mean? Just wait till tomorrow and see what happens. Looks like the bleeding's stopped, so that's good.' They both catch their breath, looking around the yard.

'Can I just ask you something else?' Jake ventures.

'Sure, shoot.'

'You said that nobody talks about your *mother* like that but you didn't say your Father too. Don't you get on with him?'

Shane rests his forearms on his raised knees and head bent, looks down at the rough concrete ground. Jake thinks he looks so lonely and dejected right then that he wishes he hadn't asked him.

'You don't have to tell me if you don't want to. I shouldn't be sticking my nose in anyway.'

But Shane looks up at Jake thoughtfully before saying, with a small shake of his head.

'Jake, you can ask me anything you want. You're the only person in here that's *ever* asked me anything and I 'preciate that. And if ya really wanna know, I'll tell ya but it's a pretty boring story so don't get too excited.'

He stares off into the distance, takes a breath and starts to tell Jake the story of his life.

His dad had hightailed it when he was a little guy. One morning, he was there when they went to school and "poof" just like that gone in the afternoon when they came home. His Mum was working two jobs and was struggling just to keep their heads above water.

There was no money for new clothes or shoes and with his younger brothers and sisters growing out of them before they wore out, there was only one way he could get them and it was down to him to do it. He started shoplifting.

He hated it, he knew it was wrong but he had no choice. Being the oldest, he felt like he had to be the man of the house, so it was up to him to provide stuff like that for them.

'Is that what you're in for? Shoplifting?'

'Yeah. The guy in the supermarket recognised me, it's not hard. I do sort of stand out in a crowd and he called the cops.'

'Still, throwing you in here for shoplifting seems a bit harsh! You'd think they could have given you a warning or something.'

'They did. But it wasn't my first time, don't forget. They've always been really good in the past and I didn't want to let them down but I was stuck.'

Jake understands. He'd felt that way often enough himself and he really feels for him.

But if he needed money that bad, why didn't he just get a job? He opens his mouth to ask the question but Shane jumps in first.

'And before you say it, I have tried to get a job but I can't get one anywhere. I've been to over fifty places in the last year but nobody wants to hire someone like me.' He motions to his face and shakes his head in despair.

'Over fifty places knocked you back because of the colour of your skin? No way! I'm sorry, mate. Sounds like it was a full-time job just trying to find work.'

'No need for you to be sorry, you can't do anything about it. But in the end, that's the real reason I'm stuck in here. I got bail but after Mum's paid all the bills and everything, she could fly in air easier than she could find money for bail.'

They're interrupted by a rogue basketball rolling over to their feet. Shane picks it up to throw back to the players but they've obviously lost interest and are walking away, sharing a fag. He tosses the ball from one hand to the other and turns to Jake.

'OK Buddy, 'nough talk. D'ya wanna shoot some hoops?'

'Nah, I'm useless but you go ahead.'

Jake sits watching Shane effortlessly land hoop after hoop, from all different angles and distances from the goal! He looks like a dancer the way he moves and Jake feels a pang of jealousy. He's always wanted to play like that! He thinks about how guys like Shane end up in here because of bigoted, petty bosses not hiring him and useless, petty salesmen dobbing him in to make themselves look good.

If they only took a minute to find out why but they didn't. And that, added to the colour of his skin, will be why Shane will never get a job anywhere. He's really had a gutful of racial discrimination over the last twenty-four hours! First the Nazis with the Jews and now Australia 2022 with all the Shanes. Will there ever be an end? He's got to do something to help him but what?

An idea starts to take shape, there's *definitely* one place he knows that would welcome this guy with open arms. And his dad just happens to know the owner of that company!

He waves to Shane, telling him that he's going inside to ring his mum now and walks off. Shane watches him go and thinks all the talk of his family must have got Jake thinking. Jake goes up to the guard on the front desk and asks when he could ring home.

He can't believe how much he's missing his Mum and he is due another call today anyway. The weary guard hands the cordless phone across to him, after checking and logging it on his computer and Jake dials his home number excitedly.

He didn't realise he was holding his breath until a sigh of relief escapes his lips when his mother answers the phone and not his dad. He wants to run his idea past her first, he doesn't know how his father will react to him asking for a favour and he's nervous to find out!

'Hi Mum, it's me!'

'Hello darling, what a wonderful surprise!'

He quickly outlines his plan to help both Shane and indirectly his mum and family and hesitantly asks what she thinks his dad would make of the idea.

'He's right here, I'll put him on and just for the record, I think it's marvellous!'

Jake quickly tells his dad all about Shane and his circumstances; how he's looked for work all year to no end and all about their conversation today. So far, his father seems to be listening intently and Jake hasn't heard anything that could alert him to any kind of disapproval whatsoever. It's then that he proposes his solution finishing with, 'Do you think it would be worth running it past Mr Harrison?'

His father tots out the old, 'Nothing ventured, nothing gained!' And promises to ring him after dinner when he's sure he'll be home. 'When will Shane be out? Do you know?'

'That's the second part of my plan!' The guard taps his watch and frowns at him so Jake quickly speeds through the rest, words bumping into each other in his haste to tell him all of it. But by the time the call is finished, his father has agreed to pay both their bails as well as finance Shane's legal fees, although when Shane is working, he'll have to reimburse him for the lot.

'He will Dad! And if anything happens that he can't, then I will!'

His father says he'll hold him to that and says he'll get it all organised tomorrow so that hopefully they can bring him home on Sunday.

*

He feels like a kid at Christmas with the growing anticipation of talking to Danny tonight. He wants to let him know that his old friend Ernie had stepped in to help them out and saved him from a beating as well, getting rid of that rotten mob; he'll be pleased to know *that* he's got no doubt. But most of all, he wants to talk to him about Shane and to hear what he thinks about his budding plan to help him.

Danny listens to Jake's account of their near miss with the thugs and Ernie's help.

'He didn't yell or shout at them, he just said what he wanted to say but *quietly;* you know, like a tough guy in a Spaghetti Western or something. But they all got the message and scurried off like the filthy, dirty rats they are.'

'Good old, Ernie! Always there when you need him, always will be.'

'Yeah, I reckon he's my guardian angel in here; oh, apart from *you* of course!'

'Of course!' Danny laughs. 'And how's Shane?'

'He's OK now, I think. He had a split lip and a cut on his forehead. So much blood! But it eventually stopped bleeding and he seemed alright when I left him.'

'Yeah, head injuries do that.'

'But I've had an idea,' he outlines his plan, which he calls Operation Shane in his own mind and fills Danny in on his parents' willingness to be involved.

'I can't believe they'd do that for someone they don't know. I mean, Mum would but Dad? Never!'

He grins, waiting for the inevitable trip down history lane to prove his point but to his surprise, Danny just nods his head and says, 'Your parents should be very proud of you.'

Jake's waiting for the *"and,"* and feels a bit confused and cast adrift when Danny merely picks up his book and starts reading. So, he reaches for his own diary.

*

Dear Diary.

Day Five, Friday.

Well, with Ernie's help I escaped a beating in the yard today.

My friend Shane was being attacked by a gang of idiots who think they're tough just because they're in a gang and I tried to get him away. When they turned on me too, Ernie just walked up and stood there. They all started shaking in their boots but he just stood there dead still and so strong.

It was like he was made out of stone or something! He even sounded threatening to me and I've never seen Ernie even cranky, let alone violent. But in the end, I don't care how he did it, it worked. It was actually funny though, watching them all take off like scared rabbits!

Like I told Danny, it feels like Ernie's some kind of guardian angel to me or something.

When I think about it, I've been lucky with the guys I've met in here.

But back to Shane and I've had a great idea! I asked Dad to talk to Mr Harrison to see if he'll take Shane on. He thinks he might! That would be awesome! I reckon Shane'd be stoked if he did and I can't wait till tomorrow to see what happens.

I know I've been telling you that I'm learning all these different things but this time, I really get it. I know Shane's going to feel good and so's his mother when Shane rings to be picked up but I actually feel good too. Not in a plaster it all over Facebook kind of way, just happy that I've been able to help someone and it's all been my idea without having to be asked or pushed into it.

It's a new idea, causing good stuff. And I reckon it's a lot better than causing trouble all the time!

Oh well, off to bed.

Good night, Diary!

Chapter Sixteen
2022-St Ives

Jake looks around in bewilderment at the familiar setting and realises that he's back at home. And it's tonight! He hasn't travelled back in the past. His mum and dad are sitting in the lounge room, oblivious to the television blaring away in the background, lost in a pretty deep sounding conversation.

He walks closer to them to hear what they're talking about. His stomach drops when he hears the worry still evident in their voices as they sit there talking about him and what's going on with his life. As usual, his Mum's sniffling away into her handkerchief but to his surprise, his father's trying to soothe her with an arm around her shoulders rather than telling her to snap out of it.

Jake's shocked to see his father treating her so gently and feels his heart break just that little bit more.

'I just keep thinking of him as that cute little boy, always ready for a hug and a kiss except when Simon was around, of course. Then it was just, "Mum"!' she pauses and they smile at each other remembering it as if it was yesterday. 'I never dreamt he'd end up in jail!'

She breaks down again and his dad quietly shushes her, promising everything is going to be alright in the end. Jake has never seen him so gentle with her before and just for a split second, envies his mother because if his dad ever had been like that with him, he doesn't remember it!

'OK. Come on. Enough of that. Just look at the bright side. We're picking him up on Sunday with his mate, Shane.'

'Yes we are and thanks again, Geoff for helping him out as well. You really are a good man, Geoffrey McMullen even though you try your hardest to hide it!'

'Yes, well,' Geoffrey harrumphs, 'it certainly would have been cheaper to bail Jacob out when he first went in and hadn't even met Shane yet!'

'Oh, stop it. It was a very nice thing for you to do.'

'Don't worry, "nice" doesn't come into it. I've told Jacob that if that boy doesn't pay me back then *he's* going to! And to be fair, he has agreed to that, offered it as a matter of fact. And Harry's agreed to meet with Shane next Friday and give him a try-out, so I just hope he's as good as Jacob says he is. I'd hate to get the poor boy's hopes up for nothing.'

Harry Harrison is the owner of the Monarchs—Sydney's top first grade basketball team. Born Horatio Gilbert Harrison, he'd quickly become known as Harry to all and sundry not long after he started school and he's known the McMullens since Jacob was a toddler.

Jake's not worried about teeing this meeting up between them as he has every faith in the whole six foot, eleven inches of Shane to make the grade and he can't wait to introduce them all on Sunday and for Mr Harrison to see Shane in action on Friday.

'I'm just so proud of him for wanting to help somebody else for a change and for putting Shane ahead of himself!' Diana smiles and Jake tears up at this and silently vows to make up for everything he's ever done to her if it's the last thing he ever does apart from reimbursing them if Shane lets them down.

But even though he hasn't known Shane for very long, he's pretty sure that it won't come to that. He'll have to work it all out somehow as he's already promised to reimburse Mr Peasey for his car and nearly choked when he heard how much they'd paid for it!

What was he thinking taking it for a joy ride like that, wiped out on bourbon and Dad's *good* whisky to boot? But that was the point, wasn't it? He wasn't thinking.

He looks around the house and sees it all with fresh eyes. Thinking back to the filthy streets of 16th century London, as well as the living conditions for workers in 19th century Sydney, he aches to feel the spongy carpet under his feet, the comfort of his favourite recliner chair and the security and love of his family all around him.

He walks into his bedroom and feels sick to his stomach when he compares it with the rat-infested basement in Ambrose Ross' *mansion*. He looks at his soft, comfortable bed and images of being chained to the wall all night vividly jump to life again. He can't believe that he was complaining about *this*.

He thinks again for the umpteenth time that having a ten o'clock curfew seems like such a paltry punishment now after the beatings he'd been given by that foul old man and don't even start on what happened to Ann Boleyn. The knot in his stomach when he'd witnessed that was still there with him today and he had a feeling it would be for a long time to come.

The tears come unchecked both with sorrow for the poor girl and also with relief that his was such a fleeting visit and he didn't have to live the rest of his life like that.

He continues his quiet and unnoticed tour through the home he'd known all his life. His parents had built this home from the ground up and they were the only family to have ever lived under its roof. He recognises now how hard they had to work and scrimp and save to be able to do it and acknowledges for the first time in his entitled life what good people they actually are.

He walks through the hall to their bedroom and notices how shabby their bedspread and floor rug are. They don't care how much money they spend on their kids or Shane for that matter but they'll keep their old things forever before they'd ever spend a penny on themselves.

He loves them accepting and helping Shane the way they have and can't help comparing it to the disgusting racial discrimination he witnessed on Kristallnacht in the streets of Germany or even this week in the exercise yard where he'd had to shield Shane from being bullied and beaten almost to death. Seems like nothing much changes in the long run.

He walks back into the lounge room just in time to hear his father say:

'I don't care what he does, he's definitely going to get some sort of job when this is all over! And he's also going to make a solid plan for the future and work out just what he wants to do with his life. No more coasting along and hoping for the best; you've been too soft on him, Di. Now it's my turn.'

'Go right ahead!' Jake thinks, knowing that he's going to be in for a big surprise! He's already decided on the course he wants to take whenever he gets out. He knows he wants to help other young kids find their feet; the way Danny has helped him but he's still trying to figure out just how he'll do that.

If the Great Crash had taught him anything, it's the value of a dollar and the importance of a good, steady job. He thinks he'll have his US dollar framed and hang it on his bedroom wall! It can be a constant reminder of exactly what it feels like to be unemployed and homeless.

He looks back at his parents again and feels so grateful for all the years of hard work they've put in to give him and Chels, the home they have. There's also a newfound sense of gratitude for the education they've given him, even though it's an education he knows he'll never finish now. There's no way the school will take him back, even for his final exams.

No, he'll just have to find another way to do what he wants to do. Maybe Danny will have a couple of ideas. They say you can do courses in prison to help you when you get out, maybe he'll look into that.

His initial feelings of warm familiarity and safety have faded into the background as he's been wandering around trying to piece everything together. He's starting to feel more like this visit has been somewhat of a rude awakening. He really wishes he hadn't done what he did and yearns to be free again to go home and start this next chapter of his life.

But he knows he has to work his way through the judicial system first, so even though he'd made these grand plans, he might have to wait years before he can set the ball rolling. He's happy that he can see a purpose to all the lessons he's had and now realises that understanding and practicing one of these on its own is not enough.

He can see how they all intertwine and the benefits to be had by the entire package. Maybe that's the end of his lessons, maybe they just all culminated in this last visit. Maybe. But he wouldn't bet on it. He's sure he's not going to be let off as easily as that.

Chapter Seventeen
2022-Mountview

'What have you been up to today?' Danny asks as Jake saunters back into the room and collapses on the bed. As usual, Danny's engrossed in his latest book and Jake thinks this is how he'll remember him, sitting on the bed, book in hand, when he's back at home waiting for his trial.

He's not dumb enough to think he'll be put back in with Danny after the sentencing, as he now accepts there'll be no escape for his stupidity this time and more than likely, he'll end up either back here or worse!

'Nothing much. Shane and I played some table tennis and then I watched him shoot some hoops, training he calls it now.' He smiles, 'I just hope Mr Harrison gives him a fair go. I had a good talk to Ernie about the "good old days" too. Boy, the things he's seen and done. Unbelievable!'

'No visitors?'

'No, I thought Mum might have come in today but she's probably at home dusting and cooking up a storm ready for the "prodigal son's" return. Hope she doesn't get *her* hopes up either!' He stops for a moment, thinking about his poor old Mum and the toll this is all taking on her and feels the stabbing nausea of guilt taking hold again.

'But talking of visits, she's got no idea that I paid *them* a visit last night!'

'I thought you might have.'

Jake fills Danny in on everything he saw and heard and how he'd seen another side to his father. Soft, gentle and caring. He'd always wondered what his mother saw in him but now he thinks he gets it. He also tells him, albeit reluctantly, his plan for reimbursing Mr Peasey and his father.

"Reluctantly" because he doesn't want Danny to think he's either currying favours or looking for praise. He really is only driven by the need to compensate for what he's done and he also knows that, while the car can be fixed, it'll never be the same again and Mr Peasey will never look at it in the same light again. How can he ever make up for the upset and trauma he's caused them?

As soon as he gets out, he'll have to get a job quick smart to start paying everything back both to the Peaseys as well as his father, especially if Shane lets them down but he trusts that he'll do the right thing. And hopefully, if this try-out is successful, that'll set him up for the rest of his life.

Danny's been listening intently and while he sees that Jake has put a lot of thought into the immediate future and how he's going to compensate and help all the others and that's only a good thing, what's going to happen after that?

'That's all great, mate but have you given any thought to the rest of *your* life? You don't want to end up back in here again!'

'Oh no. Don't worry about that, no way *I'll* be back. I'm going to follow your lead!'

'What do you mean?' Danny asks, looking up quickly frowning and suddenly alert.

Jake looks at Danny's worried face. 'What do you think I meant? It's just that I've learned so much this week because of all your history lessons and I never thought I'd hear myself say that because I hated it at school, it was so boring! But you've made me understand how it all relates to your own life. 'I'd never even thought of that before but now I get it. So, I thought I'd study history and find a way to use it to help other kids who are in trouble, just like you did for me!'

'And how do you plan to do that; once you've finished all the studying?'

'I'm not sure yet. I could be a teacher. It'd be great to get the kids to see how they can actually make it come alive and not just have to listen to some old guy droning on and on about the World Wars or the Whitlam Dismissal all day.'

'Yeah, get the little blighters *interested*!'

'That's the plan! I know I'm not as good a storyteller as you are but I must have my own way to get it all through to them; guess I'll just have to find out what it is. But don't worry, I'm not counting my chickens. If I can't make it into teaching, maybe I could be a counsellor or youth worker or something! I don't know. I'll have to work it all out later. But first of all, I've got to do all the study and courses that are needed. So, one thing at a time, eh?'

He's sure there will be TAFE classes he can do or maybe even re-do Year 12 at school and get his Higher School Certificate this time so he can still go to uni. But whatever course he takes, he's going to work his socks off to get it.

He had seen some pamphlets in the TV room spruiking tech courses available to them during the time they're here. He figures it'd be better than wasting his time out in the yard every day or watching TV and might just give him a head start when he gets back home.

Danny watches Jake's face and can see his determination and the multiple possibilities running through his mind as clearly as if it was written in a neon sign above his head. He firmly believes that young Jake will be able to overcome any obstacles in his path to achieve what he wants to do and feels very happy if he's been able to help him along the way at all.

Danny understands only too well what had happened. Jake was young and he was at the stage where he'd thought everything and everybody was against him. He felt stuck, so he'd lashed out, drinking and getting into all sorts of trouble just to prove his independence. But underneath, he knows Jake's a good boy and he's sure he'll grow into a good, solid man.

'Great idea!' he says encouragingly, 'And for what it's worth, I believe you can do it! You know, I remember reaching that same point you were at that night. You feel like all the stress and resentment has been building and building up, until one day it just explodes and you think "No more!" My father was a very quiet, private man but my mother was what you might call a "party animal". The house was always full of loud people drinking champagne, scotch; whatever they could get their hands on and I felt like I was just being crushed in the middle of it all.'

'So, what did you do? I'd scream bloody blue murder!'

'Nah, I usually just went to my room and—'

'Read history books!' Jake finishes.

'Exactly. But after a while, I'd usually creep back down the stairs to the kitchen and Mrs Fisher, our housekeeper, would always give me something to eat and drink. I'd sit there, crying my eyes out, telling her how I wished she was my mother because she was the only one who ever treated me as if I was really wanted.

'But then one day she told me something that I've never forgotten. First of all, she told me to stop crying and dry my eyes and then she said that never wanted to see them again or any more of this "dreadful self-pity" either. I wasn't still a little boy on Mummy's knee and I should start growing up!

'And then she said, "Daniel, always behave the way you want other people to behave around you. If you want to be treated like an adult, then you'll have to start behaving like one. Talk to your father! Tell him how you feel but no more whingeing and whining while you do it. Stand up straight, look him right in the eye and talk to him. And mark my words, he'll listen. Now, finish stuffing your mouth. I've got a dinner to get ready for that mob." And you know what? I've kept to that ever since.'

Jake realises that Danny's right. He's got to stop acting like the spoiled brat he's always been. He's eighteen now and it's time to man up. 'Yeah, you're right. And it fits in with something I've decided to do anyway. First thing on the list when I get home is to get a job. I'll have to study part time because I can't pay Dad and Mr Peasey back just by studying, can I?'

'Nope, don't suppose you can! But think about what sort of job you're going to look for first and just remember you're not going to be able to be too fussy to start with, after being in here.'

'Oh. I don't really know what job I'm going to look for. I haven't thought that far ahead yet. I guess just something where I can earn money while I'm studying for what I really want. I don't care what it is!'

'You don't care what? OK but be careful what you wish for!'

Chapter Eighteen
Saturday-Mountview

'Wakey, wakey!' A loud voice seems to be blasting him from the depths of a foggy, early morning dream. Mum? What on earth? It's still dark. He must be dreaming and then everything falls silent and he relaxes for about two more seconds! 'Come on! Up and at it!'

OK, so he's not dreaming. 'What, who?'

'Come on, you're dreamin'! Get up!' Someone starts shaking his shoulder roughly. Jake sits up, rubbing his eyes and looks up at the guard standing over him, shining a torch in his face.

'What's wrong?' he flinches, protecting his eyes with the back of his hand.

'Nothing's wrong, pretty boy. What, did you think you were here for a holiday? Think again mate. You're in the kitchen today! Downstairs in ten minutes and I don't mean eleven!'

He storms out and leaves the door open behind him, letting in some early morning, dark grey light from the windows around the top of the walls.

Looking at the clock, he sees that it's only 5:00am and it's before the lights go on, so he has to dress in the semi-darkness. He looks over towards Danny's bed and thinks he can barely make out his lumpy form under the blanket. How on earth can he sleep through all of that? As he closes the door behind him, he checks the time. He's got three minutes to get down there, so he'd better hurry.

As he runs, he just keeps thinking, 'How on earth do they think *I* can help in a kitchen?' He's never even boiled an egg before, come to that he can barely boil water but he guesses he's about to find out. He pushes the door to the kitchen open and is met with a wall of agitated noise, feverish activity and harsh white light.

People are rushing from bench to bench and he wonders why kitchens all have to be so noisy and disorganised. He remembers Cook, Lilian and the other servants in Macquarie St seeing that nothing really changes! And thinking of Cook, he's looking around wondering who he's supposed to report to when, right at that minute a massive lumberjack of a guy comes striding towards him, wiping his hands on a tea towel that's tucked into the elastic of his waistband.

'Jake McMullen?'

'Yes, sir.' Jake is shaking in his boots!

'Name's Col and cut the "sir" crap. You're in 'ere for breakfast. Got any experience?'

'No, my Mum did all the cooking. And Dad did the barbecues. I could wash up or something like that.' Maybe offer an alternative, he thinks, it can only help.

The guy lets out a mirthless chuckle and looks at Jake as if he's from another planet.

'We don't do "washing up" kid. That's what dishwashers are for, hygiene regulations. Another bloody beauty!' he mumbles to himself, shaking his head but still loud enough for Jake to hear. 'You can go on prep with Mike and then you can help dish it all out to that bloody hungry mob out there.'

Jake's stomach growls.

'And *we* eat whatever's left over *when* we've finished! *MIKE*!'

A tall lanky guy looks up and Col tells Jake to go on over to him and, 'Listen to what he tells ya, OK?'

'OK.' Jake nods and makes his way over.

Mike hands him packet after packet of bacon and he has to separate all the rashers into large baking dishes. When four of them are full to overflowing, he asks what he can do next. Does he want him to cut the tomatoes in half? He remembers that's how they're served every morning and thinks he'd be able to do that, no sweat.

'*Cut*? Are you jokin'? You're not getting' your dirty hands anywhere near no knife!

'Ave ya forgotten where y'are? No first timer's gonna be wieldin' bloody knives around in this kitchen!'

The other men in the kitchen all snigger and smirk at Jake's astonished expression and he turns bright red as he feels himself welling up. But then he hears Danny's voice clearly in his mind saying, 'If you want to be treated like an adult, then behave like one!'

He squares his shoulders up and tries to look unaffected, replying with a slight shrug of his shoulders that Mike's right, 'First timer. I'll get the hang of it.'

'Right, then start butterin' those bread rolls. Pull 'em apart and use the plastic spatula; you do know what *that* is, dontcha?'

'I guess it's this?' He picks up the yellow plastic blade and looks at it as he turns it over front to back, hoping it'll be strong enough to cut through the butter. But he needn't have worried about that, the "butter" is margarine, an oil-based spread actually and it's so soft, it's almost liquid. He sets about lashing it onto the bread under Mike's watchful eye.

'Hold it! God, what do ya think ya doin'? We've gotta stick to a budget in 'ere, stupid. Not so thick, just smear it on like this!' He grabs another roll from the bag and pulls it in half in the blink of an eye. Then, smearing what Jake believes to be no more than a hint of spread onto the bread, he shoves it in Jake's face. 'Like this! Got it?'

'Yes, si—' he stops himself just before the "Sir" but thinks this guy would probably revel in it anyway, he seems to have a pretty high opinion of himself. He gradually works his way through the enormous bag of rolls, wiping the spread on and then wiping it straight back off again.

When he's finished, he hears the rumblings of hundreds of pairs of feet clomping across the tiled floor, chairs scraping and the soft drone of morning conversation filling the air.

Col comes across to him. 'Right, out you go. Just follow Bazza's lead and you'll be right.'

For the next hour and a half, Jake stands behind the counter slopping one spoonful of runny scrambled eggs onto each plate while the next guy dishes out the tomatoes and so on.

Bazza's at the end giving each guy a bread roll and as Jake sees the supplies running low, he starts worrying that there won't be enough left over for them to have their breakfast at the end of the shift. He's starving!

But when Ernie pops up in front of him, Jake totally forgets about his anxiety and "accidentally" gives his old mate a double serve of eggs at which Ernie winks his thanks before moving on. Bazza's eagle eyes have noticed this but since he also has a healthy regard for old Ernie, he decides to keep shtum.

By the end of breakfast, Jake's starting to feel decidedly squeamish. It's not just the constant eggy smell or even the stale odour coming from Mike standing next to him in line but it's the constant procession of rotten toothed grins and shaking hands that are playing a big role in his nausea.

He's never had to deal with people like this before and certainly never had to *serve* them and he frowns thinking why, of all the jobs he could do, did he have to get this one? Couldn't he have done something more suitable? Like in the office or something.

He feels degraded and so sick of the sight of all the pleading, watery eyes, he decides to leave the leftovers for the rest of them and get some chips and chocolate from the snack machine.

It'll take most of his money but just this once won't hurt.

Col couldn't care less when he tells him and just says, 'Good, all the more for the rest of us!'

'What time do I have to be back for lunch?'

'Ya don't, mate. Got more newbies ta break in then! That's it for you for today. You'll get paid $3.50 fer this mornin'. See ya next week, ya'll prob'ly still be 'ere!' He laughs at his own wise crack and walks away.

*

'How'd you go this morning?' Danny asks later that night. They're back in their cell, door closed on yet another day. His experience working in the kitchen was both sickening and off-putting but at least it filled in the morning!

Jake tells him about his newfound respect and understanding for what goes on in that kitchen and no wonder the food is so on and off. 'But I felt like a square peg in a round hole the whole time!'

'It's just because you've never been in a kitchen before. Sometimes they can have huge brawls back there, so think yourself lucky it was quiet this morning for a change.'

'Yeah, it was quiet alright. But ahh, I don't know how to put this.' Danny looks at him expectantly and Jake looks back embarrassed and shame faced. 'I just felt like it was all somehow beneath me. All these toothless, rough old men and skinny spaced-out guys lining up for their breakfast and holding out their plates like they were begging or something.

'And their eyes! I can't get rid of the sight of all those hungry eyes just drilling into my face, one after another after another! I didn't think we'd ever get to the end of the line. And that's not all. I don't think some of them had even had a shower for days. I couldn't handle it, mate. I just haven't been brought up like that.'

Still a touch of the private school snob then, Danny thinks and feels sorry that Jake doesn't seem to have any compassion at all for those guys, young and old alike.

'Have you ever thought that some of those hungry men might keep re-offending just to get in here, because they've got nowhere else to go? And living here with a warm, comfortable bed and three meals a day is infinitely better than sleeping in the streets and starving?'

'Are you *serious*? Aren't there *charities* they could go to? Wouldn't that be better than being in *jail*?'

Noticing the curl on Jake's lip as he said the word "Charities", Danny recognises that young Jake still has a lot more growing up to do, regardless of what act he's putting on today.

'Charities can only do so much, Jake. They can't provide this level of care to all of the people who need it all of the time!'

'Well then, why don't they just get jobs and pay their own way? Like the guys in the Great Depression did. They wouldn't have taken *charity* if their lives depended on it!'

From the way Jake speaks, "charity" is not just a word to him but a word that should never be uttered. Danny's pretty sure he doesn't quite grasp the concept in any way, shape or form.

'You know what? I think a job *with* one of the Charities could be just the thing you need! Not to mention, it'll stand you in good stead with your sentencing once that comes up.'

He sees Jakes ears prick up at this and holds up a hand. '*Not* that that's a good reason for doing it! I just think that once you're there and meeting the people who need the help, you might get a better understanding of why they're there and where they've come from.'

'Have you ever done it?' Jake thinks it's always easy to give people advice when it's not something you would ever do yourself!

'Sure, all my childhood until I was about sixteen. My mother liked to show all her friends just how "charitable" she was and so she hosted a big kid's Christmas party every year on the lawns in front of the house for the village kids. As usual, she went over the top; pony rides, circus performers, gifts for every child and more food than some of them would eat for the rest of the year!

'You know, thinking back now, the mothers of the children would all stand to the side watching the kids and I can still see them pulling their thin coats around their bodies to stay warm. You know that self-serving show of wealth probably only made them feel even more ashamed that they couldn't give their kids those things themselves and I bet they must've been thinking about what the money spent on that day could have done for them otherwise.

'Food, clothing, education. It all seems to have been a huge waste now but I'm still glad they brought the little ones along year after year. They wouldn't have wanted to deprive them of the fun and excitement. That *was* Christmas for those kids and that was real love from their parents.

'I'll never forget the looks on the faces of those kids, the hunger, the yearning and the happy disbelief that someone would give them all this *for free*.' He stops and looks at Jake to see if he's drawing any comparisons for himself.

Doesn't look like it so he goes on, 'The first time I worked in the kitchen here, I saw that same look in the eyes of the men in the line. I always tried to give each one of them a smile and a bit of a greeting as they got to me. Didn't cost anything and it made my day better too.'

Jake sits quietly. 'Look,' he says after a while, 'I get it. It's all in the way you look at it, right? And I know someone has to do it but I don't think I'm that person. I know I said I didn't care what job I got but even if I understand them better, I just couldn't look into those faces, week in and week out. I just couldn't work with them every day! I'm sorry but I just couldn't. I know I really haven't got it in me.'

'Ahh see, that's where I beg to differ. I know you've got exactly what it takes. You just haven't worked out yet what it is and how to use it. Let me tell you a story.'

Chapter Nineteen
2022-Surrey Hills

Jake's standing on a strange street in a strange suburb. He's resting against a wall and has his eyes closed with his face up to a weak and ineffective winter sun.

'Jake! You right?'

He opens his eyes and sees a familiar, smiling woman with long brown hair and a slight frame juggling a huge set of keys and struggling to unlock the front door of what looks like a closed café or restaurant of some description. 'Delivery been yet?'

'Mmm, not sure.' Jake has no idea what delivery she's talking about but he's pretty sure she's the first person to come to this door since he's been standing there.

'Hmm. Must have had a late night,' thinks Denise and she looks more closely at him while pulling the door open. 'C'mon then, chop, chop; we've got work to do.' What a pressure pack bundle of energy she is. People like that usually wear him out just standing and watching them.

He follows her through a dining area, past tables stacked with white plastic chairs and into an industrial style kitchen. 'Oh no, not another kitchen!' he thinks in dismay. But wow! This is what I call a *kitchen*! Looking at all the brand-new equipment and professional layout, he's struck by how spick and span everything is, so clean you could eat off the floor and while Denise ties a white apron around her tiny waist, she starts outlining what's on the menu for today. But his first job of the day will be to set all the tables up.

He walks into the dining room and flicks the light switch on, causing the fluorescent overhead lights to blink lazily to life. He lifts a chair down and tucks it under the table and as he looks up to grab the second, he sees a sign painted on the wall. "Denny's Diner".

He's heard of this, it's been on all the news and current affairs shows lately. This is the place where that woman won millions of dollars in lotto and set up a charity kitchen. Now he knows why Denise looks so familiar.

He's working his way one by one through the tables when the front door opens and a large, bearded gentleman walks in, heartily wishing them, 'A very good morning indeed, to both of you!' Jake watches with interest as Denise comes hurrying straight through from the kitchen and embraces him in a big, warm hug, only introducing him to Jake once she's disentangled herself and stepped back.

'Jake, this is Nick. And we haven't seen him for quite a while!' she wags her finger and semi scolds him while Nick chuckles saying:

'Sorry, Ma'am! Nice to meet you, Jake.' Something about his bearing and his cultured speech tells Jake that he has been a very distinguished gentleman at some point but has obviously fallen on hard times of late.

'You leave these tables to me, Jake. I'm now considered to be an expert at setting this room up. Right, Denny?'

'Right, Nick! Jake, you come with me and we'll get into the prep.' Under her expert guidance, they work together peacefully for the next hour or so, only stopping for a quick chat while Denny whips up a hearty breakfast for the three of them. Sitting back, satisfied, she declares that they've reached a standstill. 'Where *is* that bloody delivery?'

As if to answer her question, the door swings open and a young guy pushing a loaded trolley bustles through into the restaurant. 'Sorry, Denny!'

'Bout bloody time!' Denny snaps as she stands and tucks her tea towel back into her belt. Jake smiles at this, remembering Col. How different these two are in a lot of ways but then again how similar in others. They'd make a good couple if neither of them is married!

They work hard for the rest of the breakfast rush, Denise cooking, Jake dishing out and Nick clearing up until the long line of hungry, homeless people has dwindled, petering right out to the last couple of stragglers. Odd people also remain sitting at the tables, unwilling to go back out onto the streets for a while yet and Jake sits with Nick at a spare table, nursing coffees while Denise pours over a ledger and makes umpteen phone calls.

Nick and Jake speak quite easily together considering their huge age difference and Jake finds out that Nick had once been the owner and senior partner of a large law office in the middle of Sydney and is then taken aback to hear a very familiar story!

He'd invested all the company's money and his own, into "quick fix" stocks but then came the Global Financial Crisis, starting in 2007 and carrying right through until 2009. He didn't have the foresight to see that it would last that long and to be fair, his financial advisor obviously hadn't either, so instead of selling in '07 and minimising his losses, he ended up losing everything, including his wife of five years and here he's landed!

Jake is gobsmacked. The similarities to Christopher and The Wall St Crash are so striking, it's just like history repeating itself. He remarks on the similarity of the financial crises to Nick; of course, not mentioning Christopher or their unlikely meeting and Nick is impressed with this young guy's knowledge and ability to draw the parallels.

So, Jake goes on to tell him about his ambition to teach history, using examples like that to bring it more to life for the kids and maybe they'll be able to avoid these destructive behaviours in the future and make sure these kinds of crises don't ever happen again.

'They always will, mate. It's greed that drives people to push their luck with investments and no amount of education will ever eradicate that! Take it from one who knows.'

At that point, their attention is caught by movement outside and they look out of the window to see a sad and afraid little woman dithering around, looking anxiously in all directions. She looks like a vulnerable little bird, thanks mainly to the yellow nightie and brunch coat she's wearing.

'Poor old dear, looks like she's got herself lost. C'mon, let's go see if she's OK,' Nick says and they both start making their way to the door.

As they step out onto the footpath, they see a young man in a blue air force uniform walking up to her.

'Are you alright, love? What's your name?'

Gladys looks up at the strapping young stranger and tries to understand what he's saying to her but she's in such a state, she can't seem to put it all together. So, she concentrates on looking at his lips to try to make out what he's actually saying. His words count for nothing, they're all fuzzy and indistinct.

But then comprehension suddenly lights up her tired old face like somebody flicked a switch or something. He's asking her name! Of course, she thinks, she must have a name! But try as she might to remember it, nothing comes to mind and her face clouds over once again with disappointment and fear.

'Come on, I'll take you inside here. They'll be able to help you. How's that? Whoops, watch that crack!' He starts to guide her towards the door but Nick and Jake are right there.

'She'll be right, mate. We'll take her from here and see what we can find out.'

Denise has appeared at the doorway. 'What's happening out here?'

'We've got a lost girl here, Denny!'

She echoes their assurances and simply says, 'Bring her in, guys! I'll get her something to eat.'

The young airman smiles at their hospitality and after they've all thanked him for looking out for her, he walks away leaving them all fussing over her.

*

Twenty minutes later, she's sitting at a table with Nick and ploughing into the delicious omelette Denise has whipped up for her, when she suddenly looks up at him with a startled expression on her face and shouts out loudly, 'Gladys!'

'Gladys? Who's Gladys? Do you want us to find Gladys for you?' Jake asks but Nick just takes her hand gently in his and says:

'No mate, I think you'll find she *is* Gladys.'

Turning back to her, he smiles kindly and asks, 'Is that your name, love? Are you Gladys?'

'Yes. Gladys, that's my name! And oh I know I'm *not* supposed to be *here* but I can't remember where I *am* supposed to be. Oh dear, I—' She looks like she's about to burst into tears. Some reassurance needed!

'Don't worry about any of that now, love. You're safe here and we'll look after you.'

She visibly relaxes and studies Nick's face with his long white beard and flowing white hair and knows she's met him before. But of course, she'll never remember from where.

'Can you remember what happened?'

'They say I had an accident that I walked straight out in front of a car not looking where I was going, I suppose. All I know is that I woke up in hospital but I don't know how I got there and that's *all* I remember.'

Her voice breaks again and she holds up a purse with shaking hands. 'Look, I've got this! There's money in it but nothing else, nothing with my name or address or,' she stifles a sob. 'And another thing! I'm sure I've got a family somewhere but oh, I just don't know! What am I going to do?'

Jake is still sitting at the table hanging on their every word but when Denise comes out from the kitchen and asks if Nick will be able to look after Gladys while she and Jake get the lunches ready, he reluctantly gets to his feet.

'Of course, I can,' Nick answers. 'It will be my pleasure!' So, Jake is left with no alternative than to follow Denise back into the kitchen and start peeling and chopping.

*

'How are we going to find out who she is and where she lives?' he asks out loud. Jake is feeling so sorry for the poor old thing. If she's been hit by a car, it's not her fault that she's here and thank heavens we're here for her and she's safe. And he thinks as he continues chopping, it's not Nick's fault he's here either; that's down to his bloody financial advisor.

He starts to wonder about all the different people who come here for help and what stories they could tell if anybody just took the time to ask. If that's just two examples, then maybe he has been a bit hard and judgemental in the past. He's overcome by a warm, excited feeling of wanting to help them all and Danny might have a point, he thinks this could turn out to be *very* good for him in the end.

As he attacks the onions, he sheds a little tear but this one has nothing to do with the stinging gases from the innocent little brown vegetable on the chopping board in front of him. Yep, definitely not the reason but it is giving him an ideal cover!

Nick walks in to make another cup of tea for his charge and smiles softly.

'She's convinced herself that she knows me from somewhere and thinks it's from David Jones' department store when she was still a young girl! She's been rambling on about a blue tea set that I ended up getting for her. You know what, if thinking that makes her happy, then I'm just going to let her keep right on thinking it. No harm done. But I've had an idea from something else she said that could help us find her family.'

He quickly outlines what she's told him and asks if Jake could make a couple of phone calls after lunch. He can't stay around today as he has something else to do this afternoon with a doctor at the hospital and he'll try to find out anything he can about her while he's there.

They leave Gladys sitting at the same table and bring her some lunch, telling her not to move. If she needs anything at all, just let them know. So, while they're busy dealing with filling a new line of empty plates, a young girl sits down with Gladys and Jake watches them starting up a conversation.

'That's just Sharon, she's in most days,' Denise tells him. 'At least Gladys is not sitting there alone.'

He nods and is just enjoying the warm sense of comradery the scene brings and thinking how great it is that they all look out for each other the way they do, when he's both surprised and angered to see Sharon grab Gladys' purse from her hand, push her roughly to the floor and make a dash for the door.

He yells at her to 'Stop!' while he takes off across the crowded dining area and crash tackles the little thief to the ground just before she makes her escape into the street.

'What the hell do you think you're doing?' he demands and calls back to Denise, who's helping Gladys up off the ground, to ring the police. 'You bloody little creep, she's a sick old woman!' He wrestles the purse back out of her grasping clutch and keeps her detained while the other diners either look on in shock, cheer him on or snarl at him for interrupting their lunch and turn back to their plates full of food.

'You stay with her and don't let go until the police get here,' Denise calls, 'they're on their way.'

'Here,' he calls back. 'Denise, can you give this back to Gladys?' He thrusts the purse out in her direction and as she gently puts it back into Gladys' bruised hand, she rubs her back reassuringly in an effort to calm her down. The poor old love is breaking her heart but after a while, she settles under Denise's calming influence.

After the police have bundled Sharon off to the local station, the place resumes its previous peaceful air and with the lunch crowd slowly dissipating, Denise sits quietly with Gladys and waits for Jake to make his phone calls. He walks back in, somewhat dejected and looking over Gladys' shoulder at Denise, he gives a small shake of his head which she interprets as "No luck!"

He pulls his chair out and knees bent, has almost planted his backside in his seat, when the door opens and Nick walks in with a strange woman in tow. She quickly looks around and lets out a little cry as she spies Gladys huddled over her table with Denise keeping watch. She rushes over, arms outstretched, crying out, 'Mum!'

She wraps Gladys in a huge embrace, crying and laughing at the same time, enormously relieved and happy to see her mum sitting there, alive and well. Gladys just looks confused.

'I'm sorry. Do you know me?'

'Mum, it's me, Ann! I've been looking for you everywhere, are you alright?'

Nick has told her about the accident and that it looks like her mum has wandered out of the hospital, hence the nightie. He'd got Ann's name and phone number from the nurse's desk, who told him that her mum had had a very nasty bump to the head and even though she's still a bit confused, she's going to be OK. But they'll have to take her back to have her checked over again before they can release her properly into her daughter's care.

'Oh, of course,' she'd said, anything to get her mum back. And now she has.

'Come on, Mum. You'd better say goodbye to everybody and don't worry, I'll get everything fixed up. You'll be right as rain in no time.' She turns back to them with a huge smile. 'Thank you for all helping Mum so much and thank you, Nick, for taking the trouble to find me.'

'You're welcome,' they all chorus as Ann starts shepherding Gladys from the dining room.

But halfway to the door, Gladys stops and pulls her arm away from her daughter's grip, looks around at Nick and beams, 'Thank you for your kindness, Nick and it was so good to catch up with you again!'

To which Nick replies, 'you're very welcome, Gladys, happy I could be of help. And I'm really glad you liked your blue toy tea set.'

Jake and Denise look at each other, eyebrows raised, *TOY* tea set?

Gladys turns to him with a smile that nearly splits her face in half as Ann tries her best to work out what they're both talking about! And as Ann walks her mother to the door, they can hear Gladys clearly saying, 'Nick gave me a lovely hot lunch and I'm feeling a lot better already!'

The door swings closed behind them and Jake and Denise both turn to Nick.

'So, *Nick* gave her all the meals then, did he?' Denise laughs, 'And found her *toy* tea set, which by the way, how did you know it was only a toy? She didn't say that before! Not that it matters because her *Nick's* such a *good boy*!' Denise teases and Jake watches them happily banter away for the next few minutes until Nick turns to them and asks if they'll be alright for the rest of the day. He's feeling done in and he still has another few things to attend to.

'Of course, mate. And thank you for going above and beyond today. And you too, Jake! You were the real hero of the day throwing yourself onto Sharon the way you did.'

Jake blushes and when Nick asks what *they're* talking about, he just brushes it off and says, 'Tell you later.'

'Ok, then. Well, I'll be off. See you both tomorrow?'

'Yep, we'll be here,' Denise promises, muttering under her breath, 'nowhere else to go!'

'And how did he find Ann?' Jake asks as they watch Nick walk out the door, 'And what do you think that blue tea set stuff was really all about?'

Denise just shrugs, 'That's Nick. Seems he can do just about anything at all! We reckon he's a magician or something,' she laughs but as they turn back to the kitchen, they stop dead in their tracks and look at each other in surprise as in the distance, they're both sure they can hear the faint jingling of sleigh bells or can they?

Chapter Twenty
2022-Mountview Prison

'I think I just met the real Santa Claus, don't look at me like that!' He can hear himself snap at Danny and knows it's because of how ridiculous that sounded.

'Of course, you did! And where exactly did you meet him?' Well, that wasn't what he thought Danny's first comment would have been.

'In "Denny's Diner", it's a charity kitchen.'

'Hmm, makes sense. What else would he do through the rest of the year? After all, he does only work one night a year, right?' he teases.

'Ha-ha, very funny. Of course, I know he wasn't really Santa but I tell you, he was the closest thing I'll ever meet to the real one. *And* his name was Nick! What do you make of that? He used to own his own law firm until the GFC happened and then he lost everything on the stock market.

'You know, I couldn't stop thinking about Christopher! They had so much in common, it was like it was the same story all over again. The only difference was that Christopher's wife didn't leave him, even when he was out on the road looking for work. She must have been a really good person.'

'Yeah, sounds like he was lucky to have her.' Danny stops, lost in thought for a couple of seconds, 'So, what were you and Nick actually doing there apart from gasbagging?'

Jake tells Danny everything he knows about Denny's Diner. And that wasn't much, just what he'd seen on telly and from being there helping with one breakfast and one lunch. Big deal! He told Danny about all the people who were coming in looking for food and how he'd never known so many people were homeless and hungry.

'You know, it's pretty disgusting, really. In a big city like this, you just don't expect to find that, do you? Not nowadays.'

'Shane can still easily end up there, you know, if your plan doesn't come off.'

'Yeah, you're right. God, I hope he gets the job. No more shoplifting food then, eh?'

He sits quietly, staring at the floor for a while sorting everything out in his jam-packed mind. He'd always thought that if someone was caught shoplifting, that was their bad luck. They shouldn't have done it; he'd sprouted out the old "do the crime, do the time" so often that he'd ended up believing he was somehow superior and *he* would never do *that*.

No, he now realises, why would he steal food to feed his family when he could steal a Porsche instead? Idiot! And he remembers how he would look down his nose even more when he would see the odd homeless "hobo" out on the street. Why didn't they just get a job instead of begging for a lousy dollar?

Oh yes, everybody had a responsibility to look after themselves, didn't they? And the charities who helped these people were only helping to keep them down! Why should they work when they could take handouts? What planet had he been on?

He knows now that the people he's met and stories he's been told in here have shown him a different angle on the whole thing and brought him back down to earth with a thud.

'You OK, mate?' Danny's never seen Jake so quiet for so long!

'Yeah, I'm fine. Just thinking. You know, I used to think that being out on the streets was like a choice. Surely, they could do *something* to get themselves out of it. And I used to look at people who were always doing things for "charity" as do-gooders, only wanting everyone to say how "beautiful" and "wonderful" they are on Facebook. But after meeting Denise and Nick, I get it now that some people really do want to help and without all the praise.'

He tells Danny the story of Gladys and how Nick had found her daughter.

'That's when I realised that everyone has their own story to tell. Gladys had lost her memory after being hit by a car, Nick had lost everything due to a world-wide financial crisis and even here, Shane has his problems just because of the colour of his skin! Before, I would have thought of them as three more losers but now'

'Yep, in life everyone's out there trying to find their way home but some people just need a bit of help getting there, that's all.'

'And so that's what charity is, right? It isn't just about giving out handouts willy-nilly, it's about helping people to help themselves so that in the end, they don't need any of the handouts.'

Danny nods, 'Yep, you got it.'

Jake turns and reaches for his diary and that's when Danny takes the hint to shut up and leave him alone.

Dear Diary

Day Six, Saturday.

I had to work in the kitchen today. Mum will never believe it! Me in a kitchen! At first it was OK and I think I did pretty well but then I had to go on the serving line and I couldn't hack it. The men all seemed dirty and desperate.

So, when I came back up, I told Danny all about it. He didn't say much, just talked about charities and stuff. And then he told me a bit more about his mother and her friends. It's bit by bit with Danny. He's pretty hard to get anything out of.

But whatever happens, I'm glad I got to know him. And Ernie too. I've only been here a few days but I feel like I know them both pretty well now and it's weird but I feel like I've known them for years.

Anyway, I ended up working in that charity kitchen, Denny's Diner. The lady who runs it is called Denise, that's the Denny part and she works in there herself and bloody hard too, all day. Before, when I'd seen her on TV, I thought she was just making herself look good because she'd won all that money and she'd have a manager and staff doing all the work but no!

She does it all with only volunteers to help her. And then in came this old guy called Nick. He'd been a lawyer but ended up losing all his money and his home and even his wife. But instead of getting bitter and sitting around all day whingeing, he goes in there to help other people. I would have thought he was crazy before but now I'm totally gobsmacked.

He helped with another old lady in there. A soldier brought her in and it turned out she'd been hit by a car. She couldn't remember anything except her first name, Gladys and she thought she had family somewhere. Nick went and found her daughter and it was great when she came in and picked her up.

I would have worried about her otherwise. Someone already tried to rob her and right in front of our eyes! I was furious and crash tackled her, keeping her there until the cops came and took her away.

Yeah, I wanted to look after that poor old girl and I really want to stay in touch with Denny and Nick. Maybe I should volunteer there when I get out, I wonder if they'd remember me? I feel the same things about Shane that I felt about her, like protective sort of and I want to keep him as a friend and I want to make sure he never ends up on the street and out of a home.

I never thought that I'd be able to help somebody else, it was always the other way 'round, everybody looking out for me! Well, no more. First Shane and then hopefully, a class full of kids if I get to be a teacher, that is.

Can you be a teacher when you've got a record? If not, I don't think that'll be fair. I know I've really changed now, thanks to Danny. This last lesson has taught me how I looked at these poor people was wrong. I've seen that in just two meals in the diner and a random meeting with Denny and Nick.

I know I'll never turn a blind eye again when I see someone on the street, I promise. You just never know what their story might be but it does make you think. They'd all been little babies once and their mothers must have looked down at them and wondered what they would do when they grew up.

Did she think this kid will be the Prime Minister? Or a lawyer? Or a doctor? Or did she just want them to be happy? I know she didn't want them finishing up where they have and if she did ever worry about that, I reckon she'd want someone to be kind and look after them.

I hope I can keep all this fresh in my mind when I go home, that's why I'm writing it all down now before I just forget it and go back to my normal life.

But that's just it, isn't it? I'll never have that normal life again!

And it won't be Chelsea's normal life again either, 'specially in the bathroom!

But that's it now.

Good night, Diary.

*

Chapter Twenty-One
Sunday-Mountview

'Can I sit here with you guys?' a deep voice rumbles over the top of the din in the dining room.

'Yeah mate, sit where ya wanna,' Ernie answers not looking up from his plate.

Jake looks up with a mouthful of eggs on toast and grins seeing the happy, shining face of Shane grinning back. He sits down and unceremoniously starts shovelling his food into his mouth.

'Mate! Are you trying to break the World Breakfast Eating Record or something?' he teases him and Shane just grins back, bits of egg dropping from his overfull mouth. He swallows it all down in one almighty gulp and wipes the back of his forearm across his salivating lips.

'Nah but since ya told me 'bout my try-out, I been tryin' to get out on the court trainin' as much as I can.'

'But we're leaving this morning! We're going home!' Jake laughs but Shane turns to him seriously and says:

'No such thing as a spare minute when you're training, Jake!'

He mops up the rest of his tomato sauce with his bread and butter and stands up, wiping his hands on his trouser leg. 'I've got my stuff ready to go and can't wait to see Mum's face when I walk in the door! She'll probably think I 'scaped or somethin'!' He laughs the excited laugh of a twelve-year-old and says, 'I'll just be shootin' hoops until your parents get 'ere.'

Ernie and Jake sit there and watch him gallop from the room.

'He looks like a kid trying to get the last bit out of a family holiday! The last swim or the last hit on the tennis court!' Jake laughs.

'Certainly looks excited but I wouldn' know 'bout any 'oliday resorts. Never went on 'olidays when I was a kid,' Ernie says between last mouthfuls of bread.

'Oh, sorry mate. I didn't mean to—'

'Nuthin' to be sorry 'bout! Just the way it was! Anyway, I'm on perm'nent 'oliday now, aren't I?'

Jake's hesitant to put into words what he wants to say next but he doesn't want to leave it unsaid. 'Ernie, mate, just before I go, I wanted to say good-bye and thanks for everything you've done for me while I've been in here.' He blushes under Ernie's questioning gaze.

'Didn' do nuffin. Don' know whatcha talkin' about.'

'Well, I know what I'm talking about and just let me say thank you, will ya?' Jake stands and picks up his plate.

Ernie looks up at him and with a thick and muffled voice, barks, 'You just go an' 'ave a good life, Jake. An' remember this, if I see ya back in 'ere again, I won't be so nice!'

'Right. Well, maybe I will be back in here again!' he says cheekily.

Ernie looks up frowning, 'Whatcha talkin' 'bout?'

'Well, I'll have to come back in here to visit you, won't I? Would that be OK?'

'Yeah, yeah mate, that'd be good,' Ernie answers thickly.

'Good. And good luck with everything. I'll see you soon, Ernie.' They shake hands and he walks out of the room without a backward glance.

As he gets to the door, a guard comes in yelling his name.

'Er, yes? That's me.' He's half afraid, half excited about the next thing to come out of the guard's mouth. Is his release cancelled or are his parents here now?

'You've got fifteen minutes to be ready. Your father's here now payin' your bail so just be ready to go when we get to your cell. Fifteen minutes! Now scram!'

'Don't worry,' one of the bullies calls out, 'Leave his stuff there. His room's already reserved for his next visit!' he adds in what he believes to be a posh voice, imitating Jake's own private school accent.

He turns and looks over at them with disdain, 'There won't be a next time, mate! As much as I've enjoyed my stay, I won't be making a comeback!' Jake calls back in the same tone of voice and receives a stern warning look from the guard.

'You're still here, so watch your smart mouth. And you've just lost two minutes!'

Jake doesn't need any more encouragement than that; he makes his way out of the dining room and back up to his cell for the last time.

*

Fifteen minutes later, he's standing next to his bed which he's stripped down with the dirty sheets stashed in the laundry basket and the blanket folded on the end of the bed. He thinks how bare and unlived in it looks now but he knows Danny will be back there tonight, maybe with a new cellmate.

He *cannot* believe that he's feeling a bit sad and sentimental to be leaving. That is just ridiculous! He's a bit upset that Danny didn't come back from the library to say goodbye and is just deciding whether or not to leave him a note when two guards appear at the door.

'Ready?' He recognises the guard from the front desk who'd brought him up here on his first day and remembers him as a kind, fatherly type figure.

'Yes. But—'

'Don't tell us you want to stay?' The other one asks sarcastically. 'I'll have to talk to chef about the food, must be getting' too good.'

'Alright, that's enough. What is it, son?'

'It's just that my cellmate's already gone to the library for the day and I really wanted to say goodbye.'

The two guards look at each other, confused. 'Your cellmate?'

'Yeah, Danny. Would you be able to say goodbye to him for me?'

'Sorry mate, can't do that. Danny was an inmate here in the mid-fifties but he committed suicide right here in this very cell.'

Chapter Twenty-Two
Monday-Home

Jake's parents expect to see a jubilant, happy Jacob emerge from behind the locked security doors and his mother quietly dreams of him running, smiling and throwing himself into her arms but what they're met with is a pale, shell-shocked and very quiet version of their son. His father frowns deeply, assessing him over the top of his glasses.

'Are you all right, son? What did they do to you in there?' he barks and turning his anger towards the guard at the front desk.

'What? Oh no, nothing. Nothing happened, Dad. I just want to go home.'

'We will as soon as Shane comes out. I've told the guard here that I'll drop him off to his mother's house on our way.'

'Oh, *Shane*!' After what he's just learned, his mind had been full of questions, denials and sorrow and he'd totally forgotten all about Shane! 'Oh, that's good, yeah, thanks Dad.'

The door opens again and Shane is standing there, his mere presence and size dominating the room. His parents step forward and introduce themselves, 'Hi. You must be Shane. We've heard a lot about you!' while Jake stands back watching it all unfold. Shane has the good grace to hang his head in shame and Diana hurries forward, hugging him and assuring him that everything will be alright now.

'Thank you very much for helping me out like this, Mr and Mrs McMullen. I swear I'll repay you every cent.'

'Yes, well, don't worry about that right now,' Geoffrey mutters and if it had been any other time, Jake would have choked on this almost charitable reply coming from his father.

'Come on, let's get you two home.'

Shane had been prepared to get the bus home, so this offer of a lift was the second best news he'd had all day, behind the guard saying, 'Right, time to go,' and made him feel like he was a part of the family. Nobody had ever treated him so well.

But the sooner he gets home, the sooner he can see his own family and his Mum's face! So instead of arguing that he can easily get himself home, he just smiles a huge, white, toothy grin and says, 'Thanks!'

As they watch Shane walk up the drive to his front door, they see the door open and hear the shrieks and laughter of his mother echoing down the path and they drive away, smiling.

*

Jake had sat with his parents over a coffee, which was something he developed a taste for while he was away and talked for what seemed like hours about the people he'd met, the food, his mother's favourite topic, the regime and the facilities.

'And Ernie was this old guy. I ate with him every day and sometimes I watched telly with him. A real old drover kind of bloke, you know like the ones in the old Banjo Paterson poems. I don't know what he was in for but I got the feeling he'd been there for years; everyone seemed to know him.

'He kind of took me under his wing and looked out for me when I had to stand up to the bullies for Shane, they were just like the kids in the playground at school! You should have seen him, Dad, he just walked slowly up and said *nothing,* just like Clint Eastwood!

'But they all just took one look at his face and took off! Yeah, I really liked him.' He runs out of puff and settles down and the cheeky grin leaves his face, 'But he did tell me that if he ever sees me in there again, he won't be so "nice".' He pulls a face that says, "Yikes!"

'And what did you tell him?'

'Just not to worry, I won't ever be back *there* again, except to visit him. Is that OK?'

His dad simply nods his head and wells with pride.

*

Back in the comfort of his own room, Jake sits thinking about everything that had happened to him and how Danny had opened his eyes to what a prat he'd been. Somehow this strange, was-he-there-or-wasn't-he guy had been able to pinpoint the exact lessons he needed to learn and had taught them with such amazing clarity that he's sure he'll never forget them.

He can't understand how he'd even met Danny but he's sure glad he did!

After a while, a plan of action starts to gel in his muddled brain and he searches frantically through his bag looking for his diary. Inside the front cover he finds his American dollar, which he sticky taped into place before he left and he stashes that safely away until he can get it framed. A concrete reminder of everything that had happened and how it felt to earn that first dollar for himself.

He opens it to the next empty page and starts writing.

*

Dear Diary

Day Seven, Sunday.

I'm home!

Thank heavens I'm sitting and writing this in my own bedroom. Danny's gone and they reckon he's been gone since the mid nineteen-fifties! I can't work out what that all means and if I didn't have that dollar, I would have thought I'd just dreamt the whole of last week.

Danny, where are you? How did I ever meet you? Will I ever understand it all? I know I'm going to miss you but thank you for everything. I had to say it somewhere because I didn't get a chance to say goodbye when I left. I hope you can help the next kid the way you helped me.

Right, enough, that was then but this is now. I have got to make a plan to get on my feet and to pay Dad and Mr Peasey everything I owe them. I can't believe I even did that to the Peaseys. I've known them since I was little and they were always really nice to me. So, they'll have to be first and Mum and Dad will just have to wait.

Things I Have To Do.

1. Go in and see Mr Peasey and apologise.
2. Get a job and work out a payment plan with them.
3. Make a payment plan with Dad for what I owe him.

4. When they're both paid off, start saving.

Things I Want To Do.

5. Find a night course in teaching and history.
6. See Kenny and sort everything out with him. And apologise for egging
    him on!
7. Keep in touch with Shane.
8. Visit Ernie once a month; does he know about Danny?
9. Look up anything I can find out about Danny and find out what happened
    back then.
10. Look up anything I can find out about Christopher. What happened with
    him and his family?

That's all for now but I reckon it's definitely enough to start with.
Good night, Diary.

*

Satisfied with what he's written and thinking he can always add to it later if
he remembers anything else, he hides it under his mattress and changes into his
pyjama pants, leaving the shirt folded neatly in the drawer. In the course of one
week, he seems to have outgrown the full set and thinks if he gets cold, he can
always grab a T-shirt.

He opens the door and decides to leave it open tonight, he's been locked in
enough and calling out good night to the family, he turns his light out and jumps
into bed.

But sleep doesn't come easily and he lies there for a while, staring at the
ceiling and thinking about how different he feels. How can you grow up in one
week and how can you become so friendly with, what—a ghost? He thinks
Chelsea must have noticed the difference in him too because she was very shy
of him when they got home and almost hesitant to initiate any sort of
conversation with him at all.

Is she scared of what he might have become? He thinks the best thing to do would be to sit down with her and tell her all about the good things that happened in there, minus the almost too realistic history lessons, of course. Try to make her see that he's not the hardened criminal she seems to think he is.

Tomorrow, I'll do it tomorrow. And he drifts off, lulled into a peaceful sleep by the dull chatter of the TV and quiet mumbling of his parents downstairs in the lounge.

*

He opens his eyes at first light and for a minute, thinking that he's still in prison, wonders what's in store for him today. But when he sees Chelsea tiptoeing past his door and stealing a glance in, he remembers that he really is home.

Just to illustrate the point, the delicious aroma of frying bacon wafts up the stairs, into his bedroom and finds its target, scintillating his taste buds and setting his tummy rumbling and that's enough to get him jumping out of bed and down the stairs in a flash.

Over breakfast he teases Chelsea, just as he always has, until she's laughing and punching him in the arm, just as *she* always has and with the ice broken, he fills her in on his plans for the bathroom. He tells her as soon as he can afford it, he'll buy another set of drawers and they both should be able to keep it tidy with one set each.

To his surprise, Chelsea seems to get excited by the idea and eagerly agrees to the plan. Obviously, his father jumps in at this point and lays down the law that Jake is *not* buying furniture for *his* home and asks him to measure up what he wants.

His mother can find one that should work. Jake agrees but silently makes up his mind to add it to the bail money and pay him back. It was, after all, his idea.

With that all sorted, Jake hits the shower; ahh, privacy and then, over a cup of coffee to fortify him, he approaches the Peasey's front door and knocks tentatively. Jennifer answers his knock almost immediately and seeing that it's Jake, she stands aside and says simply, 'Hello, Jacob. Richard's in the kitchen, go on through.'

He hangs his head and feels like he's five years old again and in trouble. He knows he's in for it now but he also knows he just has to square off and take it.

'Hello, Mr Peasey.'

'Hello, Jacob.' Cool, almost frigid and very formal. 'What can I do for you?'

'I'm glad you're both here. I want to apologise for what I did. I know it won't help much but I am sorry about what I did to your car. I don't know what got into me.'

'About a bottle and a half of bourbon, I would say.' He's not letting him off lightly, that's for sure.

'Yeah, it was about that. Anyway, I got home last night and I realised that being away in there has taught me a good deal about myself and how badly I've been behaving and treating everyone. I've had a chip on my shoulder for a long time now but I can tell you, it's been well and truly knocked off.'

'Go on.'

'There's no excuse or even a good reason for what I did in the past but I *can* control what's going to happen in the future. That's why I came over to see you, as well as to apologise. I sat up last night trying to work out how to get on with my life from here and I just want you to know that, whenever I get finally released, the first thing on my list is to get a job and pay you back for the damage to the car; it'll probably have to be in instalments though. But as soon as I have a regular pay packet coming in, we could work out a payment plan, if that's OK with you?'

'Well, I'm impressed, Jacob. You seem to have put in a lot of thought into this, so I accept your proposal and your apology. I'm just glad your coming back won't affect our relationship with your parents, it's been a long-standing friendship for too many years to let it all unravel now.'

'I'm glad about that too, Mr Peasey. They had nothing to do with it, it was all down to me. And I am home for a while but only until the hearing. I'm pretty sure I'll get jail time but I just wanted you to know my plans for whenever I do get out.'

The Peaseys look at each other, concerned. They've known Jacob since he was a little boy and they know he's not a bad kid deep down, he just needs to stay off the booze.

'Jacob, have you thought about how you're going to put your plan into action? You know you won't get any sort of career orientated job the minute you walk out the prison gates. Not with that kind of record behind you. What *are* you planning to do with the rest of your life?'

'I'd love to become a history teacher or more likely a youth counsellor and try to help other young kids keep their feet on the ground by learning from the past and there's lots of examples I can use to do that.'

'Good boy,' Jennifer puts in, she can't stay mad at him, she never could!

Jake turns to go, thinking that this is the first time he's ever been in this house and hasn't been offered one of Jennifer's famous cookies but what did he expect, when a thought occurs to him. 'By the way, Mr Peasey, how much *were* the repairs? I have to get exactly what I owe everyone sorted out.'

Mr Peasey gives a half smile in anticipation, looks Jake in the eye and says, 'It will be around $35-40,000. Even though it was my new car, it was actually an older model; a collector's car, so it couldn't just be written off and replaced. Thank you, Jake.'

Jake physically blanches at this and coughs out a croaky, 'You're welcome.'

When he's reached the door, Jennifer calls out to him, 'You forgot this!' handing him a cookie.

She stands watching him walk off, his prize cookie in his hand and his head bent.

Weight of the world on his shoulders, she thinks and closes the front door behind her.

'Richard! Why didn't you tell him it was covered by insurance? That was mean, don't think I didn't see that wicked smile of yours!'

'Let him squirm. I'll only take the excess from him and that was bad enough but he's got to stew on it for a couple of nights to take in the scale of the damage. Don't worry. I'll ring Geoffrey now and let him know everything.'

*

Dear Diary

Emergency update.

The Peaseys were pretty good about it, I wasn't even sure if they'd let me in the door or not but Mrs Peasey didn't let me down and gave me a cookie just like always.

But the cost of fixing the damage I did will be about $35-40,000! I nearly passed out on the spot when he told me. But I don't care what it is, I'm going to pay it all back no matter how many years it takes. When I find out the finished cost, I'll put it in my new ledger and add to it what I owe Dad for bail and the bathroom cupboard, then I can work out how much I can pay back every week.

I really stuffed everything up this time, like my whole life and everything hinges on what sentence I get. I wonder if Mr Harrison needs a ball boy.

Good night, Diary! (Sort of.)

Chapter Twenty-Three
Two Weeks Later

Jake has kept himself busy researching both Christopher and Danny. He's really missing him and reading all about his life seems to bring him closer again.

He knew it was going to come up so when his Mum asks him what had happened with his friend Danny, as if it was somebody from school, he simply tells her that he'd been wrongly imprisoned, he was innocent and he'd told him he was planning on heading back to England as soon as he's released.

She seems to be both relieved and happy to hear that. Jake thinks she was always worried about him befriending a "convicted something-or-other", of course forgetting that he, himself, could be exactly that!

And if he could become any sort of bad influence later on, she'd rather he was over there on the other side of the world and not right here around the corner. Let them be pen-friends. That's what he thought!

But she just replies, 'That's a shame. In some ways, he turned out to be a better friend to you than some of those boys at that snooty school!' That was Mum, keep the peace and be happy. So that was the end of that conversation.

His searching for Christopher turns up nothing more than his name on an extremely long list of bankrupts for 1929 and he realises that he'll never know what happened to his old friend. But Danny is a very different story. He finds a great deal of information, mostly in the form of a book written by Cheryl after he died and which he'd been lucky enough to find a copy of online.

The wait for that delivery is excruciating as he's got so many questions, what on earth happened? What made him commit suicide? He'd seemed a lot stronger than that. What about his family? And so, they go on.

Ten minutes after the book is delivered, he's looking down at his copy and hoping to find some of the answers he needs within its printed cardboard covers.

He'd spent the time waiting for the book to delve into the court records of Danny's case and newspaper reports of his suicide.

However, he feels strangely hesitant to start reading it now that he finally has it right in front of him. He feels like he's prying or trespassing somehow into the private life of his friend. But the reality is that Danny's actually been dead and gone for over sixty years and the book has been published, so Cheryl had had no such reluctance to write it or share its contents. He opens the cover to Page 1 and starts reading.

Danny

'Darling, you're going to have to come to terms with it sooner or later. Danny was found guilty and lost his appeal as well. He did it!' Mrs Robertson was trying desperately to soothe her distraught daughter after Danny's final appeal had failed.

'But Mum, I still can't see him doing something like that. If he thought the wedding was going to be too expensive, we could have changed the whole thing! I would have married him in the barn!' Cheryl was inconsolable over Danny's apparent guilt and no matter how hard her mother tried, there was no way she would even leave her room, let alone stop crying. Where was she getting all those tears?

'I know, your father and I think the same thing, love. We thought we knew him so well. He must have had a brain snap or something, there's no other explanation for it. And now he's facing the consequences of that.' She sits quietly for another couple of seconds rubbing her hand up and down Cheryl's arm. 'Now come on, young Bobby Reid's coming over to dinner tonight and I think he might be going to ask you to the Spring Ball! Won't that be nice?'

'Nice? It's the last thing I want to do! All those girls pretending to have sympathy for me when all they're really thinking is that I got my just deserts. I was so cocky hanging off his arm at all the parties. No! I don't want to go.'

Her mother looks at her despairingly, 'You're going to have to see them all some time, you know and anyway, your Father and I didn't raise you to be a shirker! Come on, I don't think it'll be as bad as you imagine. After all, Bobby is so handsome! Just show them that you're not a washed-up old spinster yet!'

And so dressed to the nines on the night of the ball, Cheryl walks into the ballroom with her head held high and has one of the best nights of her life.

Meanwhile, Danny is languishing behind bars and is bored out of his mind. He decides to apply to work in the library where he'll have access to all the books he can read, if he has to read solidly for the next five years, then that's what he'll do.

His cellmate, Pauley, watches him quietly every night with his nose in his book and wishes he could read too. Then he would read those books after Danny's finished with them.

Danny is acutely aware of Pauley staring at him and the wistful look on his face so one night, after he finishes the book he's just been reading, he asks him if he would like to read it before he takes it back to the library. Pauley blushes and drops his head, confessing quietly that he's never learned how to read.

Danny feels like kicking himself. How did he not pick up on that? He looks him square in the eye and says, 'Challenge accepted! You will learn how to read if it's the last thing I ever do.' And so starts their nightly lessons.

Word gets around that, not only can the new guy read but according to Pauley, he's a bloody good teacher as well. Danny feels inspired by the number of men who come to him sheepishly and ask if he could teach them too and pretty soon, he has a regular morning class going.

When he feels they're ready, he moves on to teaching them something other than the alphabet. He starts teaching history to whoever wants to learn and he calls his classes "Learn from the Past".

*

Jake stops reading and stares at that last discovery. "Learn from the Past" eerily echoes his plan for his own future! How strange.

*

His history lessons for rehabilitating the prisoners are an outstanding success. Not only are they all learning but just the fact that they have put their time and effort into mastering their writing and understanding what the past can teach them, is giving them all a new sense of confidence and ambition for when they get out.

Danny's more than happy with this but it doesn't stop him sinking into a deep depression when, try as he might, he still can't prove his innocence. It looks like his guilt is now established and it just doesn't matter what he says or does, he's in here for five years.

Well, then he can pick up the tattered threads of his old life and try to start again. One thing he does know is that he wants to go home to England and he just hopes that Cheryl will come with him.

So, what happens next takes him utterly by surprise and leaves him gasping for breath and questioning everything he thought he knew about people. Larry, one of the guards, is giving out the mail one afternoon and as usual, he has a letter for him in the now familiar pink envelope.

'No perfume today?' Larry comments as he hands him the envelope. Danny sniffs it as hard as he can and he's right, this is the first time she's forgotten to give it a little squirt with her favourite scent. He hopes her feelings towards him are not cooling, he'll have to have a good talk to her next time she visits.

But when he opens the letter and quickly scans the five sparse lines, he feels like he's been hit by a truck. Not only does she never want to see him again but she's now engaged to that little weasel, Bobby Reid! She's sorry but she just can't get over the fact that he stole from a school.

He crumples the letter into a ball in frustration and tries to hold back the tears that are springing to his eyes. It's bad enough that she's dumped him and even worse that she's engaged to Reid but he finds it utterly devastating that she actually believes he's guilty.

He goes through the next weeks in a zombie like state. He feels like he's lost his entire future; well out here anyway, he tells himself. When he gets out, he'll just head straight back to London and his eccentric parents, everything will be OK and life will get back to normal.

But when he receives a formal typed envelope in the mail later in the week, he opens it with a dreaded feeling in the pit of his stomach. The letter is from his father's solicitors and is just to inform him, in the nicest possible legalese that, as he has brought such dreadful shame on the family name, his Father has disowned him and therefore removed him from his will. Please take this as first and final notice and they wish him the best of luck with his life in Australia.

He reads it over and over again with a shocked disbelief. He can't seem to get it through his head that he's been cast adrift without a penny. His family wasn't that great really but he never expected this!

He uses the last of his money to ring London but neither of them will speak to him. Mrs Fisher tells him that his mother has been totally drowning in shame and says if she ever sees him again, she thinks she'll have a nervous breakdown. Of course, his father just follows her lead, as usual.

It's the first time he's ever heard Mrs Fisher sound bitter and he loves her for that. Actually, he just loves her for everything. She goes on to say she's so sorry about what's happened and she doesn't believe for a moment that he did this awful thing. If he needs anything, just let her know.

It's at this point that his money runs out and he shouts, 'I love you, Mrs Fisher,' into the mouthpiece just before the dial tone comes back on. He hopes she heard him because he knows he'll never speak to her again.

A couple of days later, Larry finds Danny hanging in his cell. The note he left explains that he couldn't live with the shame of everyone he loves thinking he could be guilty of such a heinous crime and this is the only way out he can see.

Please forgive him.

*

Why didn't he just talk to somebody? Jake feels like he's been punched in the stomach. He can't believe his friend had been so desperate and nobody even noticed. He didn't *have* to die, he could have had counselling, couldn't he or could he?

He remembers clearly hearing his father talk about the good old days when men were men and there was none of this "feelings" rubbish. Maybe men were just supposed to suck it up and ride it out or else they were thought of as "weak".

Now he has to know, even more, who set Danny up because he's convinced that Danny was innocent and therefore, somebody else *must* have been guilty.

The trail linked to Danny has come to a stop with his suicide, so Jake starts looking at theft cases around that time. Cheryl has listed the names of his colleagues in her book, so that's a start. If it was a student, then that'll be a whole different kettle of fish.

Scanning through the court files from that year, his attention is caught by one name that jumps out at him and causes his heart to race with the sudden comprehension. 'Oh no, don't tell me!' He opens that file and reads the sparse details. He needs to make sure it's the same guy and so pulls up the newspaper stories from the time. The first one he sees shows a photo of Danny's happy, smiling face and a headline that tells the whole story.

"SCHOOL TEACHER EXONERATED" Colleague Anthony Copeland charged with theft.

The article goes on to tell Danny's sorry story and how he'd been let down by the justice system.

He had been kind enough to fill in for Mr Copeland when he'd taken ill, which meant that Mr Fielding had had to double his workload during this period. He did that willingly and according to the school Head Master, had achieved great success with both classes. But he'd been let down badly.

He'd firstly been the victim of the ruthless Mr Copeland and then the victim of the justice system who convicted him based purely on circumstantial evidence. Mr Fielding took his own life three months ago. He was unable to come to grips with his dire situation. RIP.

Jake sits back and stares at his bedroom wall. Poor bloody Danny. He'd obviously knocked himself out doubling his classes and that's how this creep repaid him. Why?

Why would Anthony do that? Because Danny was the new guy and trusted him completely?

He turns back to his computer when he's called down for dinner.

*

He can't get back to his researching for a couple of days as Kenny has finally come home on bail and his mother, Fay brings him over to apologise to Jake's parents while the boys have a "supervised" visit sitting in the lounge room in full ear shot of the whole family.

Both guys are very subdued and the others can see they're both scared out of their wits at the prospect of lengthy jail terms. Jake tells Kenny about his cellmate, Danny who is a real history buff and how much he learned from him while he was in there.

Kenny had not been so lucky and had been in with a really rough guy who treated him like dirt under his feet. He even goes to the point of saying that he wishes he would have died that night, it would have to be better than spending even one more night locked up in there with him.

Jake feels an almost electric shock go through him at those words and fighting the tears that are welling up in his eyes, he talks to Kenny softly, reassuring him that he most definitely has a life to look forward to and that he can do great things with that life but he can never achieve anything if he's not here to do it.

'You'll always have your family to help you and me too, mate. You ring anytime you need to talk when we get out, obviously. And I mean that for the rest of our lives. OK?'

'OK.'

Diana and Fay are both sitting weeping and Geoffrey keeps clearing his throat gruffly, to disguise his welling emotions. This is the first time he can say that he's really proud of his son and silently vows to help him any way he can for the rest of *his* life. And to think he'd been on the verge of giving up on him altogether and that's something Jake can never know.

*

When he finally gets back to his trusty computer, he comes across an old radio interview with Anthony Copeland from inside prison. The interviewer, Susan Hill is asking him why he'd done that to Danny, did he have a particular beef with him?

His answers simultaneously satisfy his curiosity and frustrate him even more, only serving to renew his anger at the selfish prat who was responsible for the death of such a great man.

Anthony:	I was told that I had to retire because I'd been takin' too many sick days off.
Susan:	What's that got to do with Mr Fielding?
Anthony:	Nah, nothin'. He was just in the wrong place at the wrong time like.
Susan:	OK but still you took the money and left Mr Fielding to take the blame. Why did you do that?

Anthony:	I needed it to retire on. Not that *that* piddlin' little amount would have 'elped much. But I'd only ever been a casual teacher because of my health and they don't pay much for that. So, I didn't have much money put aside, like. I ended up just living on what I did have 'til it all ran out.
Susan:	And that's when you decided to hand yourself in?
Anthony:	Figured that livin' in 'ere with three meals a day would win over livin' on the streets any old day.
Susan:	So, it suited you then. Don't you feel any remorse at all that he took his own life because of it?
Anthony:	Ah, don't start that! He was a big boy and it was his decision. I 'ad nothin' to do with that!
Susan:	Right. That's enough. Thank you.

Jake notices the disgust in her voice and is himself overwhelmed with that same disgust at the callous disregard he had for Danny's life. Did he really believe he had nothing to do with it? Did he honestly think that Danny would have taken such a drastic and final step if he'd been happily teaching, married to Cheryl and on the farm each weekend?

The only bit of cheering news he read was the post script at the bottom of the interview. Anthony Copeland's illness had killed him six months after this interview was recorded. He died in jail, a convicted thief and a ruined man.

So, now he knows it all. Jake wishes with all his might that he could talk to Danny one last time but he knows he'll never see him again. He will definitely use the lessons Danny taught him though, to live a better life. And he'll do this in honour of Danny's memory.

Chapter Twenty-Four
Mountview District Court

The day finally arrives for Jake to face the court. Because he's pleading 'guilty', there's no need for a protracted trial and he'll go straight to sentencing. Geoffrey has engaged a well-known solicitor and barrister for both him and Shane and they in turn have given both the boys the same advice. Plead guilty. It's the best way to go to try to secure a shorter sentence.

Jake's family arrives at the courthouse on the day of his hearing and they have some time with his legal representatives. They go over everything that will happen that day and they stress to Jake the probability that he won't be going home with his parents afterwards.

He just has to be ready for that.

'But it's not all doom and gloom.' Mr Collins, the solicitor smiles, 'Mr Peasey has advised us that he no longer wants to press charges and has agreed to appear today as a character witness in order to reduce the severity of the sentence.'

'That is good news, I'll have to thank Richard when I see him.' Geoffrey beams, 'But if he's dropped the charges, why can't we all just go home and forget about it?'

'The police were the ones that pressed the charges in the end, so they're the ones who'd actually have to drop them for all this to just go away. But Mr Peasey's statement will go a long way to helping with the magistrate's judgement.'

*

It takes a further three hours before he's finally called. Jake finds himself sitting well away from his parents in the dock and looks around at the filled seats, fiddling with his hands nervously. Shane is there, watching and waiting with nervous eyes.

He's there to support Jake as well but is nonetheless weighing the procedures up nervously, anticipating his own appearance next week. He smiles when he sees Jake looking over at him and Jake tries to smile back but knows it's more of a scared grimace than a grateful smile. Good old Shane.

Mr Peasey is called to the witness stand and gives his testimony. When asked how long he's known Jake, he states clearly and calmly, 'Almost all his life! I think he was about 18 months old when we first met the family.' He then goes on to give his impression of Jake as a kind and courteous boy, who has got into the usual kinds of scrapes that a lot of boys get into, unfortunately culminating in the theft of his car and damage to both the car and the front door.

But since he's come home, he has shown true remorse and has offered to pay for the damages he caused. He also seems to be planning a life on the straight and narrow, if he's given the opportunity.

The magistrate thanks him and hears some more testimony from various friends and family members finishing with his father. Geoffrey takes the stand and smiles encouragingly over at his son.

'Mr McMullen. Have *you* noticed similar behaviours and traits in your son since his return as Mr Peasey has just testified?

'Yes, I have. Jake seems to have matured overnight while he was away. He's come back with what seems to be a greater understanding of who he is and where he wants to go in his life than he had before. I know it was only a week but the change is truly noticeable and I must say, for the better.'

He goes on to outline how he helped Kenny the other day and believes that he will continue to keep his promise and keep helping Kenny for as long as it takes. 'And that makes me a very proud father indeed.'

Jake looks over at him in astonished gratitude. That's the first time his father has ever said anything like that to him and he genuinely wants him to go on feeling that way.

However, when he looks back up to the frowning face of the man sitting in judgement on him, he sees that he's just staring at his notes, his brows knit, deep in thought and Jake realises that he's holding his breath waiting because this man still holds his whole future in his hands and he knows the next few seconds will determine his path for the next few years.

The magistrate takes off his glasses and rubs both hands vigorously over his face and eyes with the expression of someone who's found themselves at a crossroads. Does this boy deserve yet another chance? So far, he's wasted every single chance he's been given.

But he gets the feeling that the week in prison has shown him that this is for real this time, he's not in Juvenile Court now. He puts his glasses back on and prepares to speak.

'This crime is very serious, Jacob. Do you understand?'

'Yes, sir.'

'And looking at your record, you've been given ample chances to change your behaviours in the past but have wasted each and every one of them.' Jake feels a sinking feeling wash through his entire body. Visions of what happened to Kenny in his cell run through his head and he knows for sure that he won't be so lucky with his cellmate this time.

'I've carefully considered all the character testimonials, your obvious remorse and your offer to repay for all the damage you've caused and I don't think a custodial sentence would serve any purpose at this particular point of time. Your rehabilitation away from the prison service would seem to be a lot more beneficial to all those involved.'

His hopes rise just a bit. 'Don't count your chickens,' he thinks.

'I will accept your guilty plea but won't let it be shown on your record, this time. And I sentence you to damages and court costs, time served and I'm placing you on a good behaviour bond for 2 years, to report weekly to your local police station for the first six months.

'Now Jake,' he addresses him directly, 'You must understand that if you do anything at all illegal and that means even a driving offence, for the next 2 years, you will be immediately incarcerated and your 2 years will start all over again from that date, to be served in confinement. Do you understand that?'

Jake can't help the grin that is splitting his face in two. 'Yes, Sir. I do.' And he means every word.

Outside the courthouse he's surrounded by his family and friends, all extremely relieved and all very excited and revelling in the moment. He knows he's not off scott free but he vows never to let anybody down again, himself included.

Shane comes up and Jake asks him how he's holding up? He tells him he's fine and Mr Harrison has been great letting him work there as a general dogsbody and he can train whenever the court's free, as much as he likes! The plan is to do that until he's been to his hearing and then until an apprenticeship becomes available.

He'll then be able to apply for it along with whoever else happens to apply. Shane is excited about that! Also, Mr Collins the solicitor has told him that he's not likely to go back to jail for shoplifting, so he's quietly hopeful.

That night, the family have a subdued, reflective dinner at home. But Diana announces that next week, they'll have a slap-up night out in a fancy restaurant to celebrate. Jake tries to dissuade her as he doesn't think being given another chance is anything to celebrate, it's more like something to move on from.

But she won't hear of it and madly starts listing all the restaurants she's planned to visit for a long time but was just waiting for a good excuse. He smiles at his father and they both understand that this is an opportunity for her for a night out and they both shrug, why not? He's caused her so much heartache in the last few years, why put the lid on her enjoying a dinner out now? She looks so happy.

*

So, roughly ten days later, they walk into *"Abercrombie's"*, the newest and most exclusive restaurant in the city. It's owned by a celebrity chef from a TV cooking show that Diana would never miss and they're all dressed up to the nines in anticipation of a great dinner.

They're escorted to a table set for four by the window and even though it's dark outside, the view is magnificent taking in all the city lights and the busy, restless streets glittering and alive with red tail lights.

'It looks like a fairy wonderland!' Chelsea enthuses. She'd pictured these fairy lands so often when she was a little girl that she'd actually recognised this scene as one of those!

'Bit old for fairies, aren't you?' Jake teases but there's none of the old animosity between the two and their mother beams at the two of them getting along so well. Geoffrey, however, has missed the entire interaction with his head buried in the menu and his mind filled with possibilities. Everything looks so delicious, it's almost impossible to choose.

He's on call tonight, unfortunately, so when his phone rings half way through the main course, he sighs and excuses himself to take the call.

'Looks like no dessert, kids!'

'That's OK, Mum,' they both chorus.

But after a couple of minutes deep in conversation, he comes back to the table with a huge smile on his face.

'What is it, darling?' A confused Diana asks, wondering why he's sitting back at the table grinning like the Cheshire cat.

'I have news! Shane got the apprenticeship! He had his hearing today and he only received a fine and a warning. Looks like they didn't even advertise it. I know Harry's been watching him train unbeknownst to Shane, so he must have liked what he saw.'

'That's great news!'

'Good on him!'

'Fabulous!'

They all exclaim over the top of each other. But then, just as suddenly, Jake falls silent.

'What's wrong, Jacob?' His father asks, he thought Jake would have been over the moon at this news.

'I totally forgot it was his hearing today. He was there for me and I wanted to be there for him. Some friend I am!'

'Hey, stop that right now. You've been there for him all the way. He'd still be in jail if it wasn't for you! And it was your idea for me to talk to Harry about him. He's free now, he's got an apprentice with the Monarchs and he's on the best path possible for him to make something of his life. And that's all thanks to you, son.'

Jake wells up at this and says that he'll give him a ring tomorrow. They were both so lucky that his dad had hired Mr Collins for them. They couldn't have done any better.

Geoffrey turns to Diana and says, 'And do you know what? Harry told me that Shane's asked for half of each pay packet to come to me until he's repaid me for the bail and legal help. But Harry's already told me he'll cover the legal and court costs, so he's just left with the bail.'

'Oh, that's wonderful! But you're not going to take it, are you?' Diana has always thought that once the money's gone, it's gone and there's no way they're going to miss it now!

'I very definitely am going to take it, every last cent. He has his pride, love. He doesn't want to feel he's under any obligation at all, to anybody.'

Jake shakes his head and reasons, 'But friends can do nice things for each other without obligation, can't they? I mean it's all very well wanting to feel that he doesn't owe you anything but he has a family that's been struggling through tough times for a while now.

'Dad, can you please ring Harry back and tell him not to do that? I'll pay you back for both our bail and he can pay me back when he's rich and famous with front row seats for every game!

'It might take a while before I've paid you back for everything but right now they need that money to live on and I mean food and stuff, nothing fancy! And looking around at how we're eating tonight, I think we can afford it better than they can!'

Epilogue

Jake stands in front of the college in the dusky twilight and thinks back over where he is today. The last year has been a roller coaster and that's putting it mildly. But now, with his job as a teacher's aide in the local primary school and his night course for a Diploma of Education, he's looking forward to doing something just for his own enjoyment and this history course is just what he needs.

He's been missing his "History Adventures with Danny", ha! That sounds like a good idea for a TV show in itself and he's decided that the only way to know enough about it all to teach, is to immerse himself in a course like this. This is his first day and he always feels a bit lost on his first day anywhere.

A new building to learn, new people to meet and new schedules to follow. But he knows once he's settled in, he's going to really enjoy it. It's just a shame he can't share his real/unreal visits with anybody else in the whole world. If he did, they'd lock him up again and that's for sure.

He still doesn't really understand what happened or why it happened, back there in the jail but he knows he certainly learned enough from it all to turn his life around. If he can do the same thing for other wayward kids, then that will make all of this more than worthwhile and will give his life a true purpose.

He doesn't care if it's within the education system or in homeless shelters or even youth groups at the weekend but he's determined to get to them somehow. He knows that a lot of good kids only go off the rails due to unstable home lives or the lack of support and backing of the education system due to coming from disadvantaged backgrounds.

He shakes his head to bring himself back from these daydreams, which seem to be his new hobby, to the reality of the moment and starts the long climb up the front steps to the reception area. He looks around and sees that the staff have all gone for the day and wonders how he'll know which classroom to go to.

To his right, he sees a large, cork pin board with several notices and lists tacked to it and walks over to see if there's anything there relating to his course.

"History 1" is written boldly at the top of one list and that's followed by a long string of names, among them his. 'Right,' he thinks, 'Room 12.' And then immediately looks around for any hint of which way he needs to head for Room 12. Luckily, signs are painted on the walls showing room numbers and arrows pointing all over the place, so he's at least got a direction to follow.

Finally, he's standing in front of Room 12 and he pushes the door open to reveal a classroom full of students. The teacher is standing with his back to the door writing on the white board. Most of the seats are taken, no late comers here then, with only the front rows empty. Just like the school bus on excursions, he thinks. Nobody wants to sit near the teacher!

He takes a seat and pulls out his pens and writing pad, stowing his bag safely under his seat. He then swings around to the boy behind him to say hi! He'd noticed him the moment he came in and was instantly reminded of his old friend Simon, sitting there all alone while the rest of the students all chatter happily away.

They strike up a conversation, maybe even the beginning of a friendship and quickly forget just where they are, not hearing all the other conversations fall silent.

'Please don't let me interrupt you!' comes the half-joking admonishment from the front of the room. Jake swings around in his seat, blushing with embarrassment and stares up at his new teacher, his mouth dropping open in amazement.

Mr Daniels pushes his glasses back up his nose, smiles and says in a very familiar English accent, 'Good to see you again, Jake, old son!'

THE END